NATURAL RESOURCES

Shelter's voice echoed dully off the stone around him. He crouched as Coral lowered the lantern to where the light gleamed on the rocks at her feet. Shelter gasped when he saw the thin streaks of gold. "Is this typical?" he asked, unable to hide his amazement.

"I've no idea . . ."

"If it is, you'll be able to justify all of this work. If the other ore even approaches this high-grade stuff, it will be worth any trouble and expense to bring it up," Shell said, dusting his hands together.

"Now," Coral said, her head cocked to one side, "isn't that exactly what I told you, Mister Morgan?"

Shelter recognized the gleam in Coral's eyes. It was the gleam of a woman who knew how to use her natural resources to get what she needed. Right now, she needed someone to help save her mine. And if there was anything else she needed, he'd provide that too. . . .

THE CONTINUING **SHELTER** SERIES
BY PAUL LEDD

#14

SHELTER

THE GOLDEN SHAFT
BY
PAUL
LEDD

ZEBRA BOOKS
KENSINGTON PUBLISHING CORP.

ZEBRA BOOKS

are published by

Kensington Publishing Corp.
475 Park Avenue South
New York, N.Y. 10016

Printed in the United States of America

1.

The rifle shot was a sharp, rolling crack somewhere in the distance. The fat drummer on the stagecoach seat opposite Shelter Morgan lifted a pudgy finger, opened his mouth and then slumped to the floor of the coach, blood foaming from his lips.

Morgan saw the splintered hole in the wall of the Concord coach, saw the nasty black crater in the side of the drummer's skull, heard the woman beside him scream.

"Get down," he shouted at her, and when she didn't, he yanked her from the seat and pushed her to the floor of the coach where she lay with wide-eyed horror against the bloody body of the dead drummer.

A sawed-off runt of a man named Hal Trevor was driving the stagecoach and now Shelter heard his excited shriek fill the air, felt the sudden surge of the stage as Trevor whipped his team into a dead run.

Morgan slid to the window and looked out at the endless red desert, searching for the sniper. It was a time before he saw them, racing their horses after the coach, spumes of red dust flying up behind them as they laid down a barrage of hot lead.

A bullet nicked the sill above Morgan's head and he ducked reflexively. Bringing his own Winchester level he steadied it on the jolting sill and answered the ambushers' fire with some .44-40 magic of his own. A damned lucky shot plucked one of the attackers from his saddle.

It didn't slow the others a bit. Shelter thumbed fresh cartridges into his Winchester and spared a glance for the woman who lay sprawled, hat cockeyed, on the floor at his feet.

Young, dark, pretty—and scared to death. She looked up at Shelter with pleading eyes. A bullet ripping through the wall of the stage caused her to drop her head and snuggle up against the body of the drummer.

Morgan steadied his rifle and fired rapidly at the pursuing outlaws. The shooting was impossible from the rocking stagecoach, but it bred some caution in the bandits. They fell back, halting their horses before unleashing a savage volley.

The bullets ripped into the side of the coach, like the fangs of some feral beast. Shelter hit the floor as the stage raced on, the thunder of the horses' hoofs loud and near, the stage jolting into the air.

Hal Trevor screamed and Shelter glanced up to see the driver's body fall past the window, bounce off the red earth and be crushed beneath the stagecoach wheels. Still the team raced on, mindless, frothing.

"What happened!" the girl shrieked. Shell ignored her. He lifted his head and fired three shots back at the pursuing bandits who must have figured they had this job licked by now.

They had dipped down into a narrow, brush-clotted ravine and the driverless horses balked at the crossing. They swung abruptly to the right and the coach heeled over.

It rolled twice, slamming Shelter against the wall and then the roof of the stage. Dust swirled around them. The dead body of the drummer, the living, struggling body of the girl tangled with his own before the coach came to rest on its side. The horses ran free across the red desert and Shelter Morgan, dazed pinned beneath the drummer struggled to free himself.

They would be coming in now, coming hard. Shell kicked open the door of the stagecoach and yanked the crumpled figure of the girl from the coach which lay on its side, twisted and broken, a rear wheel still slowly spinning.

Morgan heard a shout before he saw the approaching horsemen and he raced for the cover of the willow brush, dragging the protesting girl after him. They dove into the willows just as the bandits crested the low rise to the east.

The girl started to say something and Shelter immediately clamped a hand over her mouth. His eyes flickered to her pretty, dirt-streaked face and then returned to the rise.

Six men. Two riderless horses. They sat watching for signs of movement, signs of life. Then they came down, riding abreast, rifles in their hands, masks across the bottom half of their faces. A big man in a red shirt riding a stocky buckskin gelding seemed to be in charge. With hand signals he sent three of his men

7

down toward the stage. They never made it.

Morgan, firing from a prone position, opened up with his Colt.

There was no doubt about the first man he hit. The top of his head was blown away and he cartwheeled back out of the saddle, his horse rearing up on hind legs. Shelter shifted his sights to the second man, squeezed off and immediately moved on to the third, the Colt bucking twice against the palm of his hand.

The second man slapped at his shoulder and spurred his horse savagely, riding directly at Shelter. The third had already fallen to lay writhing against the sand.

Shelter fired again at the approaching horseman, saw the bullet shear through his collar bone and tear the throat out of him. The gunman went from the saddle as the horse he rode narrowly avoided Shelter and the girl, running blindly through the ravine.

On the rise the guns had opened up and Shelter answered with two snap shots before rolling away to shove fresh loads into his heated Colt.

The girl touched his arm and tried to ask a question, but Shelter ignored her. He had no choice. The holdup men were coming in again. The three that remained.

The bullets cut brush around Shelter, whipping with deadly menace through the willows. Morgan sighted on the chest of the lead horse and fired. The roan buckled at the knees and went down, throwing its rider free to somersault through the air and land sharply on his neck. Shelter doubted he would be getting up again.

The other two had had enough. Emptying their weapons in Shell's direction, they wheeled their horses and rode over the rise, leaving their dead behind them.

"If we . . ." the girl began, but Shelter silenced her. He listened, and his ears told him that the riders were indeed pulling off. At least two horses were running into the distances.

"Stay here," he told the girl after five minutes. She looked angry, frightened and quite pretty. Her dark eyes raked Shelter Morgan's face as he backed away toward the ravine, then circled toward the rise.

The afternoon was hot. His boots sunk to the ankles in the red sand as he clambered up the rise, throwing himself to his belly as he reached the crest.

They were gone. The desert stretched out toward the whitish playa to the south, toward Mexico, and in the other direction lapped at the base of the saw-toothed mountain range which ran north and south across the land, bleak, forbidding, lifeless.

In the far distance Morgan saw what might have been two horsemen walking their weary animals toward the north, but it might have been illusion. Heat veils rose up from off the desert flats at this hour, mocking vision. Between himself and the playa there seemed to be a glimmering blue lake. There was no lake and hadn't been for eons.

Shelter got to his feet, feeling light-headed, parched, weary. He looked at the stagecoach, the dead men surrounding it, the wounded horse which still moved feebly in its death run.

Above him were the chocolate brown hills of the Dragoons. Dry wasteland populated only by rattlers, scorpions, coyotes and jackrabbits. And somewhere far beyond the hills lay the town of Rembrandt and Morgan's grim objective. Death upon death. It was

9

endless and sickening. His life seemed as dry and empty as the broad desert.

He wiped back his dark hair, holstered his Colt and walked down the sandy slope to where the woman waited.

She stood dusting the sand from her buckskin-colored skirt. Her hat had been lost and her dark hair hung unevenly, the right still being dressed with ringlets, the left tangled into a somehow appealing snarl. Her small nose was smudged. There was a scrape on her left cheek. At Shell's approach she stopped her primping and stood hands on hips, watching him, her firm, small breasts rising and falling beneath her white blouse.

"Are they gone?" she asked.

"Gone."

"We should find Mister Trevor. He might need tending to." She looked momentarily puzzled. "He fell off back there, didn't he?"

"He fell off, but he won't need any tending to," Morgan said.

"Oh." Her voice was weak, her eyes studiously avoided the dead scattered about them. The injured horse still struggled and Morgan, shaking his head walked to it, placing the muzzle of his .44 next to its ear before touching off. The roar of the gun was loud, echoing up the flanks of the chocolate hills. The horse lay still.

"I think I'm going to . . ." the girl began, and then her legs gave out. She hit the ground and Shell crouched over her, holding her head on one knee until she came around, staring at him dazedly. "I fainted!" she said.

"You did." Shell grinned.

"I! How womanly!" she said with genuine anger.

"No it's not. It's purely physiological," Shelter told her. "Anyone can faint. If I had the time, I'd faint myself right now."

"You're mocking me."

"Never." Morgan helped her to her feet. She staggered slightly, and Shell had to place his arms around her. She fought him for a moment before surrendering.

"Independent little thing, aren't you?" he asked, still holding her to him.

"I've had to be." She looked at him curiously, her head cocked to one side, her dark eyes glittering. Then she said, "I can stand up now."

"All right." Still it was a moment before he let her go. She stood looking at him then broke away, the pulse in her throat dancing with an indefinable emotion.

She watched as the tall dark haired man with the piercing blue eyes turned to walk toward the stagecoach which lay on its side uselessly.

"Crazy bastards," Morgan muttered. He had searched the boot and the box, finding no strongbox, nothing of value. "What in hell did they think they were after?"

"They weren't looking for a strongbox," she said.

"No?"

"No. It was me they wanted."

"You?" Shell's eyes narrowed. "Why is that?"

"I can't tell you that."

Morgan only shrugged, turning away to remove his hat and wipe his brow with his cuff. "There's a sorrel horse down in the ravine somewhere. Or there was.

I'm going to see if it's still around. You might look through your own luggage and see what you want to take."

"We're going on to Rembrandt—together?"

"I'm going on to Rembrandt," Shelter said a little roughly, "and I intend to be mounted on that sorrel horse. If you'd prefer riding to walking, then yes, we're going together."

The girl nodded and Shelter turned away, mentally shrugging. A funny kid with a funny name. She had introduced herself to Morgan and the drummer back at Soccoro. Coral Scant. The drummer had made some kind of joke. He looked back across his shoulder at Coral, wiped the sweat from his eyes again and trudged down the ravine, searching the heavy brush for a frightened sorrel horse.

Coral Scant watched him go, then she turned to her baggage which had been thrown free of the coach as it rolled and which now lay some fifty feet upslope not far from where a headless bandit now lay. She kept her eyes averted. It wasn't the first dead man she had seen in the last months, and she supposed he would not be the last, but she didn't have to look at them, to think about it, did she?

Inside her trunk was a small valise packed with undergarments, mirror, brush, comb, hairpins and powder. She took that from the trunk and placed it aside. Then, slipping her hand into a sidepocket built into the trunk, cleverly concealed behind a false panel, she removed the little chrome .32 revolver, looking over her shoulder toward the ravine where the tall man searched for the sorrel horse.

She slipped the pistol into her skirt pocket. "No,

Mister Shelter Morgan, I don't trust you very much. We'll be travelling a ways together. I hope we both make it to where we're going."

Still there was a lingering, pleasant memory of his strong arms around her, of that impossibly ingratiating grin and she half-smiled before, closing the lid to the trunk, she walked back to the stage to wait in its shade.

Morgan was grumbling curses, fighting his way through the tangle of sage and manzanita, nopal cactus and yucca, chasing the sorrel which watched him warily, allowing Shelter to approach within arm's reach only to suddenly bolt, to run fifty feet and stand watching again as the man approached, mumbling those strange, dark words.

The heat was stifling. There wasn't a hint of a breeze in the ravine. The sun was a white ball floating through a white sky. Twice he stepped on a barrel cactus and felt the saberlike pain of the heavy thorns cutting through his boots into the tender flesh of his foot.

And the damned horse seemed to be making a game of it! Shell stopped, looked upslope, unable to see Coral from where he stood, worked his way around a stand of ragged gray boulders on a treacherous slope, and came up on the sorrel again, talking soothingly, pleadingly.

Eventually he caught the dangling reins and the sorrel gave up its game, seemingly happy to have a man take charge again.

Shell looked upslope, stepped into leather and started that way, his head drumming with pain, his throat and chest soaked with sweat.

She sat there cool and quite young-appearing,

hands clasped in her lap, small satchel beside her, watching Morgan break free of the brush to ride up to where she waited.

"Ready?" she asked brightly and Shell said he guessed he was. The outlaw had not carried a canteen or else it had been lost in the battle. Shelter's throat was dry, his tongue stuck to his palate. He helped Coral up behind him and turned the sorrel westward with only a last glance backward at the dead, at the wrecked coach.

The sun followed them as they rode through the mountain pass, following the stage road toward Rembrandt. Coral said nothing to him. Morgan's head continued to hammer. He had some sore ribs on the left side and his left thumb had been jammed rolling around inside the stage. Coral had her arms around his waist, but her grip was decidedly tentative. Fine.

Shelter couldn't have cared less, although she was a damn fine looking woman. His thoughts were elsewhere as they crested the hills and were suddenly overlooking the town of Rembrandt.

There—somewhere below—was the killer, and Morgan would have him. He would have him or die himself. It had been a long road, but it ended here on this red desert for Able Sharpe.

2.

Rembrandt, someone had named the town. Shell doubted Rembrandt would have wanted to paint it. Likely it would have offended his eyes. It stood squat and dark in the late shadows before the rising foot-hills. A dozen false-fronted frame buildings stood along Rembrandt's only street. The road was rutted, dusty, uneven. Beyond the town was a narrow creek, probably the reason for the town's existence. Water was hard to come by in this area.

"That's it, is it," Shelter said musingly. He shifted in the saddle. Coral, holding on to his waist tentatively gave a small wordless answer. She might have been only clearing her throat.

"Is this your home town?"

This time she answered. "Since I was six." It seemed there was acrimony in her voice.

"Don't like the place?" Shelter asked. "Or is it the people?"

"Are we going on down?" she asked sharply.

"Yes." Shell kneed the outlaw's horse and it started

forward eagerly down the long barren slope, perhaps knowing that a stable and hay awaited it at Rembrandt. It was probably not the first time this horse had seen the town. Morgan planned on keeping a sharp eye out for the other horses he had seen that morning. One, a thick chested buckskin, he would know on sight. The horse and its red-shirted rider, the man who had been in charge of the ambush.

Rembrandt rose off the red desert as they approached. Dusk was settling in and the street and hills beyond the town were shaded to a deep violet. Lamps began flickering on in various windows. In the general store the shades were being drawn as the storekeeper closed up, anticipating an evening meal, a quiet evening at home.

Shelter was expecting nothing like that.

He would have to see the sheriff if Rembrandt had one. The danger of being seen by the escaped stage robbers was strong. There were few towns across this stretch of desert—it was likely that they had their base in Rembrandt.

And there was the man.

Able Sharpe was here somewhere, waiting to kill or be killed. Shelter was here to make sure it was the latter.

"Where's the sheriff's office?" Shell asked across his shoulder.

"Why?" there seemed to be a note of panic in Coral's response.

"Why? We'd best report this, don't you think?"

"No." The panic was definitely there. Shell halted the horse in the middle of Rembrandt's empty street and half turned to face the dark eyed girl.

"Why not?"

"I just don't want it reported. There's no sense in it. The sheriff can't do anything now."

"How do you know that?"

"I know it." Her voice lowered as a pair of cowboys emerged from a restaurant, picking their teeth. They stood looking at the horse in the middle of the street, at the tall, hard looking man and the pretty young girl in a dress that was definitely not cut for riding. "They'll find out anyway. Why should we be involved?"

"You mean let them figure it out when the coach never shows up?"

"Yes! Can't we get out of the middle of the street?" she asked in exasperation.

"If you tell me where to go to find the sheriff."

"I can't . . . listen, just get out of the street. I'll explain it all."

"All right." Shelter kneed the weary sorrel and it walked, head down, toward the alley beyond the restaurant. There Coral slipped swiftly from the horse's back, and belongings in hand tried to dart away. Shelter was from the sorrel's back in a flash, grabbing her wrist.

"Hold up," he said. "We had an agreement."

"An agreement," she spat. "How do I know I can trust you?"

"Trust me for what?"

"I can't tell you." Her eyes lowered and Shelter let go of her wrist. "I just can't explain," she said. "I didn't want anyone to know I was arriving on that stagecoach and I don't want anyone to know I'm here now."

"All right."

17

Relief washed over her face. "You won't tell anyone then? You won't go to the sheriff?"

"I'll go to him, but if that's the way you want it, I won't mention you. You don't want to tell me about it, do you?" he asked.

She seemed about to say something, then, deciding, she shook her head heavily. "No. I can't really, Mister Morgan. I've got to be going now," she added.

"If you're going to the hotel we can go along together," Shelter said. He was still studying this small, pretty woman trying to fathom her. She had a secret and it was a secret not to be shared. She was convinced the holdup men had hit the stage because she was on it, not for hope of any gold shipment. But she couldn't, wouldn't, explain that. All right—that was fine with Morgan. He was sorry the girl had problems, but he had his own. He was curious, but not curious enough to harass her over it.

"I won't be going to the hotel," she said, looking away.

"All right. You'll have a place to stay?"

"I have a place." Then her small white hand came up and Shelter took it in his own, finding it cool, as cool as the rest of Coral Scant. He watched as she turned away and walked up the alley, carrying her secrets with her.

Shelter found the sheriff's office two blocks up. He entered finding a lean, leather faced man with a mustache playing solitaire with a greasy deck of cards. A tarnished star hung on his leather vest front.

"Yeah?" he looked at Morgan, boots to hat, measuring him. "What is it?"

"You the sheriff?"

18

"That's me. Colin Flowers."

"Shelter Morgan. The stage west was hit ten miles back. I was on it."

"What?" Flowers rose from his desk, scattering cards. "Where's Hal Trevor. It's his job to report this, damn the little runt."

"Trevor can't report anything."

The anger seeped out of Flowers' expression. "Like that, is it?"

"Like that."

"Anyone else?"

"There was a drummer with us. Never did get his name. He caught a bullet. He's dead. There's a few dead outlaws scattered about up there. Maybe you'll be able to put a name to them."

"And you're responsible for that?"

"I'm afraid so." Shelter took off his hat and wiped back his dark hair. The sheriff was examining him more closely now. The lean face of Morgan, the Colt which rode comfortably on his right hip, those icy blue eyes which the sheriff found he didn't care to look into too deeply. "I've got one of their horses outside, Sheriff. Maybe you're familiar with the local brands."

"I am!" Flowers bellowed, grabbing his hat. "Let's have a look."

They did, but learned nothing. The brand was a Rafter CB, and wasn't local, Flowers said. "I'll look into the register and find out who's running it, but likely the horse was bought legal. We'll never trace the rider."

The sheriff stood thoughtfully studying the sorrel for a long minute as the last purple light of dusk faded to darkness as if he hoped to learn something of signif-

19

icance by simply staring at the animal.

At last he shook his head. "Can't see why they'd hit that coach. Everyone knows the westbound don't carry payroll or gold."

"They might not have been local men, Flowers. Maybe they didn't know. Or maybe they just were willing to settle for whatever we happened to have in our pockets."

"Could be." He shook his head. "Still, I don't like it. You're not keeping anything back from me, are you, Mister Shelter Morgan?"

"No, why would I?" And why was he? Why keep the woman's secret? Likely it was nothing. Maybe she was trying to avoid an old boyfriend. Maybe she was running away from family or husband. Maybe anything—but Shelter kept silent. He had said he would and that was enough.

"Where will you be?" Flowers wanted to know.

"Hotel, if I can find it."

Flowers told him how to do that and then said, "You won't be drifting real soon, will you?"

"Not tonight," Shell answered with a smile. The sheriff smiled in turn, weakly. Morgan turned and started toward the door. With his hand on the knob he halted and said across his shoulder, "By the way, Flowers, I'm trying to look up an old friend of mine. Name of Able Sharpe. Know where I can find him?"

"Able Sharpe? No, I don't. Never heard the name before, Mister Morgan."

Shelter nodded his goodbye and stepped through the office door, Flowers' eyes still on him, unreadable and morose. Outside it was already cool. The temperature dropped quickly on the desert. The pale quarter moon was rising in the east, spreading a faint pallor across the desert.

The sheriff hadn't said anything about the sorrel so Shelter stepped into the saddle, riding it toward the stable, a pole and mud affair a block west. A stout Mexican, scratching his head came forward to meet Shell and lead the sorrel into the stable.

Shelter caught the man's eyes as they went into the lamplit structure. He looked once at the sorrel, then his eyes seemed to narrow, to light with intelligence. Then he looked at Shelter and the light went out.

"What is it?" Shelter asked.

"Nothing, *señor*."

"Have you seen this horse before?"

"No, señor, never."

That was that. The man wasn't going to talk and Morgan couldn't make him. But he knew that horse. Just now Shell didn't care. He had made the holdup artists pay and he wasn't interested in any side jobs just now. Let the sheriff track down the bandits if he could, just now Morgan was interested in only one man—Able Sharpe. In the man and a night's sleep. It had been a time since he had slept in a bed. The naps you could catch in a stagecoach did nothing to relieve a man's weariness. The jolting, jouncing stage had hard wooden benches which came up every few seconds to slap the butt, clack teeth together, shake the innards. Morgan swore he could still feel the motion of that coach after three days on it.

The hotel was of two stories, with a false-front indicating a third which wasn't there. The desk clerk seemed surprised to see a live paying customer.

Shelter checked in and was shown to a ground floor

room fronting an alley. There was a window curtained with cast-off calico, a bureau with a cracked, smoky mirror, a sagging bed covered with a patchwork quilt. Shell closed the door behind the clerk and, tossing his hat onto the bureau, stretched out on the bed, watching the cobwebbed corners of the ceiling, listening to the tinny music up the street.

Another hotel room, another town, and they seemed now to be all the same room, the same frontier town. It had been a long, long bloody trail.

Shelter's mind flickered back to the beginning, the very beginning, to when he had learned what treachery was, to when a handful of men had taken whatever illusions he had and smashed them to dust.

The Conasauga. The trail had begun there. Along that dark, cold Georgia river on a dark cold afternoon. They wore the gray, those of them that had uniforms at all. They wore the gray and Sherman was on the march. They were little more than a straw curtain in the path of this Union tiger, and they knew it.

How could they not. The trees around the camp were blackened by cannon fire. The injured lay moaning, screaming in the patched tents while a surgeon without bandages, without morphine, worked over them with despair tragically lining his once-young features.

And the Conasauga ran red with their blood. The dead floated in the river, moving down to the sea.

In the distance Union campfires burned brightly. Thousands of them like fireflies in the night. You couldn't look at a man without seeing tragedy on his features, hopelessness.

Captain Shelter Morgan had enlisted out of Tennessee in the early days of the war, coming down barefoot out of the hills to take the oath. They had given him his first pair of boots, a new shirt and trousers, a fine rifle. He had felt like a king.

In those early days. It dragged on and the dead friends outnumbered those who lived and fought beside him. Morgan had been three times promoted in the field and he carried his rank well, accepting the responsibilities without assuming the snobbery which was present through much of the officer corps—the old line, the aristocrats, the gentlemen.

Morgan was no gentleman. He was a warrior.

"Captain Morgan?"

Shell opened an eye. He had been leaning against a broken oak, sleeping as he always did, when any small opportunity presented itself. The corporal waited patiently while Shelter stretched and wiped his eyes free of sleep.

"What is it?"

"The colonel would like to see you, sir."

"All right."

The corporal saluted and withdrew and Shell came to his feet, dusting off his tattered uniform, forming his torn hat. He strode toward the colonel's wooden-framed tent, trying not to see the dead, the dying, the pain-ridden faces.

A man with one hand saluted and Shell returned it. Brooks. Sergeant. One of Shelter's men. His men. And his duty was to lead them into hell, to be dismembered and clawed, killed, gutted. You didn't think about that for long.

There were unfamiliar horses staked near the colonel's tent and Shelter frowned thoughtfully. The big

23

white horse was an officer's mount, and a high-ranking officer's. Colonel Fainer had important guests.

Shelter rapped on the wooden half-frame and was summoned into the dark interior of the tent. There a lamp glowed dully. Familiar faces looked up at Shelter Morgan as he entered. The gentlemen officers, those he had never felt quite comfortable with, and who obviously felt uncomfortable with this lanky captain.

The colonel, stolid, smiling, confident, rose to greet his line officer.

"Welcome, Shell."

"Sir." Morgan nodded, looking around at the intent faces seated around the makeshift plank and crate table.

Gordon Wakefield was there, his dark eyes glittering in the dim light, and Major Twyner—the major had a large red nose and an empty sleeve. He hated the Yankees with a devoted passion. They had taken his arm already and were within five miles of his plantation at this very minute.

Leland Mason, one of the "true" aristocrats, a haughty, soft-faced man was there, Captain Reginald Bowlen who had a trunkfull of hoarded goods, an easy, meaningless smile and the temperament of a rattler when provoked.

And there was Able Sharpe. Lean, dark, seeming to match his name. Quick intelligence flashed in his eyes as he met Shelter's gaze. Intelligence and faint mockery. Able Sharpe was another aristocrat. Twelve thousand acres of cotton in Alabama.

In the corner sat the man with the star on his epaulette. The colonel said, "Captain Morgan, may I in-

24

troduce General Custis."

Shelter bowed mechanically, taking in the clean and pressed tailored uniform of the general, the piercing green eyes, the meticulously barbered silver hair, the lines etched around his eyes, at the corners of his mouth.

"Sir."

"Now," Fainer went on heartily. "If you'll be seated, Shell, the general would like to speak to you."

Morgan, shrugging mentally, took a seat on an empty barrel.

The general, looking cool and confident stood hands clasped behind his back.

Morgan nodded amiably and waited for the general to begin. Custis was in no hurry to do so. Finally he seemed to make up his mind and he turned sharply to face Shelter.

"You're up from Tennessee, I understand."

"Yes, sir. I'm from a town called Pikeville."

"Which is near Chickamauga," the general said. He was slowly lighting a thin cigar, talking around it.

"Just a stone's throw away, sir."

"We were run out of Tennessee, Morgan," Custis said. "It was a bitter defeat we suffered at Chickamauga."

"Yes, sir."

"I was there, you know. Yes, I was there." The general watched the smoke from his cigar rise in bluish wreaths toward the tent roof. "Do you know Lookout Mountain?" the general asked suddenly.

"Lookout? Yes, sir. I know most of that country. I climbed Lookout as a boy." Shelter could still recall it. He had climbed the mountain just to get a look at the

25

country. Just for the sheer pleasure of standing on the rocky crest and looking out at those blue hills, at the lazy river wandering.

"I assume that you know all those backtrails then? The ridge routes?"

"I know them as well as any man," Shelter answered. "It's been a time, but I recall them well."

"I see." Custis was silent, thoughtful for a moment. He and Colonel Fainer exchanged a glance. The other men in the tent either stared at their hands or at Morgan. Especially Sharpe. Able Sharpe looked hungrily, excitedly at Shelter Morgan and it puzzled Shell.

"He's the man, sir," Colonel Fainer said quietly. "I've known Captain Morgan a long time. He's intelligent and dedicated. And he's good at his work. Damned good."

"Yes," the general responded, "I believe you're right. All right, Morgan, I'll tell you what this is about. When we got pushed out of Tennessee, we pulled out in a hurry. We left a hell of a lot behind."

"Yes, sir, I know that."

"Do you? I wonder. I'll tell you exactly what we left, Captain Morgan. A quarter of a million dollars in gold! A payroll bound for Lee's Army of Virginia. It never got through. The fighting was too fierce. We had to withdraw ourselves, and damned quickly. Those of us who got out with our skins counted ourselves lucky."

"A quarter . . ."

"You heard me, sir," the general snapped. "A quarter of a million in gold. Have you any idea how much that is translated into medical supplies, musket balls, blankets and boots?"

Custis leaned nearer, the lanternlight shining in his green eyes. "We need that gold, sir. We've got the contracts, British merchants ready to supply us with all that we need to survive this winter, to feed our men, to keep them warm, to kill the pain they're suffering."

"You want me to have a try at recovering it," Shelter Morgan said.

Curtis looked at Shell, chewing on his lower lip thoughtfully. "Yes, Captain Morgan," the general responded. "That is exactly what we want. We need a man who knows that country like the back of his hand—it's infested with Union troops. We need a man of scrupulous honesty, a man of determination. Colonel Fainer assures me that you are all of these."

"I appreciate the compliment."

"It had better be more than a compliment, Morgan!" the general bellowed. "You had better be exactly what the colonel believes you to be. I can't begin to tell you how much depends on this mission."

Shelter had taken the assignment. A fool's mission, it was. With a few hand-picked man he sifted through the Union lines, keeping to the high ridges, travelling at night, and somehow, miraculously, they had reached Lookout. Even more miraculously, they had made it back. Made it with a quarter of a million gold dollars—and only a single man lost.

One man who had been told to keep his head down and didn't listen. A Union sharpshooter had picked him off. But by God they had made it!

Captain Shelter Morgan, Sergeant Jeb Thornton, Welton Williams who was fond of guns and damned good—too good—with them, Dinkum Williams, called the Dink, a mild, bespectacled and thoroughly competent man. They, by God, had beat the odds, beat the whole damned Union army.

They came upon the others in a clearing not far from the Conasauga.

They were all there. General Custis, Colonel Fainer. Twyner, Sharpe, Bowlen. Twenty of them in all, officers and enlisted men alike. And they were all wearing civilian clothes.

Shelter reined up, his horse shifting nervously, perhaps sensing something. As Morgan did. Shelter looked at Custis who was immaculate in a white linen suit and white planter's hat.

"Is the war over, sir?" Morgan asked quietly.

"It's been over for a long time, Morgan," the general replied. "Anyone with eyes to see could tell you that. We've had our butts whipped."

"And you figure it's time to get out now." Morgan was looking at each man in turn, imprinting their faces on his memory, for he knew now. Knew what his mission had been about and it had nothing to do with war or compassion.

"They want the gold," Welton Williams had said to his captain, and Shelter glanced at the dark-eyed gunhawk, nodding.

"So it seems. Is that right, General? Colonel Fainer, sir? Is that it?"

"Shelter . . ." Colonel Fainer said in what was almost a whisper. "The war is over, man! We all know that. A few more months at the most, then we'll all be surrendering our weapons. We'll be paraded off to camps. And then what? We'll go home to our burned homes, to places where we won't even be able to vote or have a voice in our destinies. The old South is dead, son! We've fought long and hard for a just cause, for our freedom. Well, the cause is lost. Let us have something for the tremendous price we've paid and will continue to pay. Let us start again!"

"With this gold."

"That's it."

"That's what we went through hell for? To deliver this gold to you who are going to desert your men when they need you most? No, sir. We took an oath! Maybe you don't remember it, but I do. Not only that—what you told me before is true—we have hundreds of people who aren't going to make it through the winter without medical supplies, without blankets and food. They'll not live long enough to lay down their arms without help, and you damned well know it! Your rationalizations don't amount to a hill of Georgia manure beside that, Colonel. I'll not hand this gold over. If you're going to run, get the hell out of my sight."

"Shelter—" the colonel seemed genuinely regretful. "You have no choice." He swallowed hard. Morgan simply stared at him, cold blue eyes glittering.

Fainer had been his friend, his commanding officer, his sponsor. All right—his idol, the man Morgan had admired most in the world. Fainer had led them through hellfire, through storms of grapeshot and musket balls, never flinching, never saving himself. Now he was displaying cowardice for the first time in Shell's memory. He was afraid. Afraid of facing defeat.

"Don't force this, sir," Morgan said.

"There are twenty of us," Lieutenant Able Sharpe had said savagely and Morgan turned his head to stare at the man.

29

"I don't really give a damn if there's a hundred," he answered quietly. "This isn't exactly the first time I've faced an enemy."

"Shell, be reasonable!" Fainer pled.

"Sir. I'll do what I have to. I always have, and believe me, I always will."

The colonel did believe him and he had to look away. A horse shifted its feet, a crow croaked in a blackened oak tree. Shell's mouth was dry, his every sense alert. And then it happened.

Who started it, Shell never was to know. Possibly Welton Williams who lived to become a savage, crippled man. Williams who had a shady past, who fought with two pistols and unerring eye. Who was to meet Shelter again, much later on another trail when Welton Williams, rising up from the grave a madman, tried Shelter Morgan on for size.

The guns exploded, detonating the silence of the Georgia morning. Gunsmoke rolled across the clearing. Horses went down in thrashing, bloody heaps. Jeb Thornton, stolid, courageous, loyal, was blasted from the saddle before Shell's eyes. An injured bay horse did a macabre dance on Welton Williams' chest, crushing him. Dinkum caught a bullet in the face, another in the shoulder and Shelter screamed: "Ride!"

Dinkum had, flopping low across the withers while Shelter held them back for a minute, his gun blazing, before Morgan himself was tagged and he rode out of the ring of death clinging to the mane of the big horse he rode, the bullets singing all around him, the gunsmoke searing his nostrils and eyes, the hot blood trickling out of his wounded body.

Later he found Dink dead. Later still the boys in the

30

blue uniforms had found Captain Shelter Morgan, CSA, still living, but barely. They had patched him up and thrown him into prison on spy charges, having been captured in civilian clothes.

What were those prisons like? Later everyone would hear about Andersonville. No one mentioned the fact that thirty thousand Confederate boys died in Union camps. Shelter was not among them. He survived—perhaps it was the fire of hatred burning in him that kept him warm through those long winter months. The war ended and still Morgan was held.

Lee himself was set free and still Morgan was a prisoner. Spies, after all, do not deserve the honor of pardon.

There were seven long years of deprivation, of seeing nothing green and growing, of watching no woman's skirts lift as she stepped from her carriage, of eating nothing but gruel and rancid meat.

The questioning Shelter was occasionally subjected to indicated that they thought he knew something about the large quantity of gold missing at war's end. Shelter always believed that someone had informed, wanting him kept in prison for as long as possible.

Because they knew.

They knew that when Shelter was freed, nothing in this world could keep him from coming after them. That day in the clearing three good soldiers had been murdered. Three of their own. They had in truth killed hundreds of others by taking that gold. Those who froze to death that winter, those who starved or died from the lack of medical supplies.

Those men—Custis, Fainer, Sharpe and the others —trusted leaders, had grabbed what they could and they had run. They had taken an oath, but the oath meant nothing to them when they saw the opportunity to profit by the war. During those long years in prison Shelter had taken his own oath.

They would pay.

They could scatter to the winds; they could run but they could not hide. They owed a debt and Shelter Morgan was going to be behind them to collect it.

It had been a long and savage trail. Most of them had come West where there was room to hide, where the law was thin and scattered. But there was Law. The law of the gun, and Shelter Morgan was its enforcer.

Shelter's eyes flickered open and he stared for a long while at the gray ceiling of the hotel room. Rembrandt, Arizona, and it was time again.

Time the Law came home to Able Sharpe.

3.

Shelter slept until nine. Then he went downstairs and out into the street. Rembrandt was dark and mostly silent. In the two competing saloons, however, there was life and light. Shell started toward the first, noticing the sign which offered sandwiches. He had a hunger gnawing in him.

He had a second reason for visiting the saloon. He was looking for a man. Although the sheriff had never heard of Able Sharpe, or claimed he hadn't, Morgan knew he was here somewhere. And if he was, someone could point him in Sharpe's direction—willingly or unwillingly.

Benny Dierking had been a soldier. He had been with Shell in Georgia up until the last. It was Benny who had told Shelter in Soccoro that Sharpe was in Rembrandt. That was just the night before Benny had been knifed in a Soccoro alley.

The saloon was a glare of light, a wall of noise, the harsh jangling of a tinny piano, the shriek of a woman, the crash of glass, a smoky room, a dozen card games, the stink of unwashed men and stale liquor.

Shelter eased on in, his eyes searching the room carefully. He bellied up to the bar and waited until the harried bartender in the greasy apron worked his way down to where he stood.

"Beer. Sandwiches?"

"Don't know if there's any grub left," the bartender said, wiping the bartop, drawing a beer and accepting Shell's change almost in one motion.

"Will you see?" The bartender nodded and continued to work his way down the bar. Shell hadn't thought there'd be many cattle in dry country like this, but most of the men he saw wore chaps and spurs, had rough, leathery hands, all the marks of cowboys on them.

The bartender returned with two ham sandwiches. The meat was cut thickly, well-smoked, the bread yeasty and stale. "Thanks," Shelter said. "Seen Able Sharpe—I'm supposed to meet him here."

"Don't know him," the bartender said. Then he was away, slapping mugs onto the counter with both hands as the cowboys clamored for their drinks, shouting and cursing.

Shelter chewed on his sandwich slowly, finding that it tasted just about the way it looked. It was filling, however, and that was what mattered.

"Buy one for me?" the woman at his shoulder asked.

"You hungry?"

"A drink, silly."

"All right."

Shelter looked her up and down. She was on the far side of thirty, this blonde with the world-weary eyes, wearing a red dress with a few burst seams along the hips where the material clung tightly. Her milky, full breasts tried to push their way free of the material where it plunged downward in never-ending cleavage.

The bartender somehow heard her order above all the others and in seconds there was a greenish drink in a fancy glass before her and Shelter was short two dollars.

"We can sit at a table," she suggested.

"All right." Morgan picked up the other sandwich and his beer mug, following the woman across the room to a table which was occupied already by two tired-appearing bar girls.

"Clear out, Clara," the blonde said and the others rose, winking slyly.

"My name's Sally," the blonde said, sagging into a chair opposite Shelter. He still chewed thoughtfully on his sandwich. Swallowing, he introduced himself.

"Shelter Morgan."

"You a cowboy?" Sally asked, her eyebrows drawing together.

"No."

"I didn't think so, somehow." She sipped disinterestedly at her anemic drink.

"Just passing through. I was supposed to meet a friend here, but I can't locate him."

"No?" Sally's head turned as a fight broke out in the far corner of the saloon. Two cowhands throwing windmill punches at each other worked their way across the room, scattering card players. The bartender broke it up by stalking toward them with a club as thick as his forearm. "Boys," Sally scoffed. Then she sighed again. "Nothing but boys. I'm glad to meet

35

a real man."

"The man's name is Able Sharpe."

"What man?" Sally's face went blank, her pale blue eyes emptying of intelligence. "Oh the one you were supposed to meet. What was that name?"

"Sharpe. Able Sharpe."

"No. I never heard it before, and I meet most of them from time to time. But not many like you." She leaned her elbow on the table and cupped her chin in her hand. "You busy later, Shelter Morgan?"

"Later?"

"After this joint closes."

Shell, looking around him, wondered if the place ever closed. The two cowboys had made up and were best of friends again. "No," he answered, looking Sally up and down again, finding her over-ripe, but still pretty, still alluring. "I'm not busy. What time do you get off?"

"Midnight. When I want to, and I want to to-night."

"I don't want to wait around here," he told her. "I'm over at the hotel. Maybe you'll be able to drop in."

"Oh, I'll be able to drop in," she said, and her hand dropped to his thigh, giving him a slight squeeze before she patted her hair and sat upright. "You want to talk a while more?"

"I've got a man to look up," Shelter reminded her.

"All right. It's just as well. The boss gets mad if we talk and the customer doesn't buy us drinks." Shell was starting to rise and she caught his wrist. "You'll be there? You won't forget?"

"I won't forget," he promised.

"Good." That satisfied her and Sally stood too, walking to a cowboy who had just entered as Shelter, smiling, went out through the batwing doors and into the street.

He paused, looking Rembrandt over. Nothing stirred outside of the saloons and he decided to cross to the competing establishment. The moon had risen, casting black pools of shadow before the buildings, a crooked, lean shadow against the red earth street before Shelter.

He had no more luck at the second saloon, the Continental as it was called. He had another beer, talked to a few more men who had never heard of Able Sharpe and went out again. He was beginning to wonder if Benny Dierking hadn't steered him wrong.

The simplest explanation, of course, was that Sharpe had changed his name. Most of those he had tracked had done just that. He had described Sharpe to people, but a description doesn't really mean much to most folks.

Sharpe: tall, dark, middle-aged, sharp-featured. Shell himself had seen a dozen men that evening who easily fit the description. Morgan shrugged his shoulders against the chill of the desert evening and started up the plankwalk toward the sheriff's office, wondering if Flowers had had any luck with the stage robbers, wanting to pump him again about Sharpe. And, truthfully, Shell was curious about Coral Scant. Maybe without breaking his promise he could somehow discover who she was, where she had gone, why she didn't want it known that she was back in Rembrandt.

He had the opportunity to do none of that. The sheriff's office was locked up tight. A prisoner in a back cell was singing a melancholy song off-key.

The weariness had begun to settle by the time Morgan headed back to his hotel room. He remembered Sally then and the promise in her eyes. The recalling of her full, milky breasts, the way her tongue darted out to moisten her lips set Shell to stirring, and he realized he wanted her badly, needed a woman on this weary, chill night.

Back in his room he washed off in the porcelain basin and stood shirtless looking out his window at the rising moon. Then, turning the lantern down to a mere flicker of light, he stretched out on the bed, hands behind his head, watching the ceiling and those damned bloody heads which kept appearing up there. All the dead and dying, all those he had met on this long and bloody trail.

There had been the war and its years of bloodshed, then prison, now this endless vengeance trail and Shelter wondered if he would ever have any sort of normal life.

He must have dozed off. The lantern had burned itself out and he was sitting up in the darkness, Colt in hand, and someone was rapping softly at his door. He crossed to it and swung it open.

"Hello."

Sally stood there smiling uncertainly. The light from the hall cast an aurora around her yellow hair. In the shadow and light she was lovely.

"Come in," Shelter said.

"I thought maybe you'd changed your mind."

"Why would I?"

"I don't know." She stepped in, closed the door behind her and fumbled with the knob.

"There's no lock," Shelter said.

"Oh, well." She shrugged and crossed the room, studying the lanky man on the bed. "A little light?"

Shell nodded and she walked to the bureau, turning up the wick in the lamp, striking a match. The lantern glowed softly behind her as she turned, hands behind her back and began unfastening the buttons of her dress.

Shelter watched her slip out of it and stand in her chemise facing him. Then that too was gone, followed by stockings and garters, until Sally stood naked before his approving eyes. Her breasts rose and fell as she filled her lungs with deep inhalations. Shell let his gaze shift to her sleek, long thighs, to the patch of down at their juncture. He lifted a hand.

"Come here."

She crossed to the bed, sat on it and leaned back, her head on his chest as his arm snaked around her. His hand found and cupped her full breast, toying with the taut brown nipple.

"Do you like me?" she asked, rolling back her eyes to study Shell's face.

"Sure."

"I could tell you did. Right from the first."

She straightened up, rolled onto the bed, straddling him on her knees. She tossed back her yellow, disarranged hair and her hands went to the buttons of Shell's trousers. Her lips puckered with concentration as she gradually undid them, allowing Shelter to spring free.

"Oh, my," she said, biting at her lip. Her hands encircled his erection, her thumbs tracing inflaming scrolls around the head of it. Shelter slowly unbuttoned his shirt and cast it aside.

Sally sat back and tugged off his pants, her eyes glittering now. She was intent on her work, not noticing the smile which played across Shell's lips as she yanked his pants free and came down to him, her breasts flattening themselves against his hard-muscled chest.

She nipped at his neck, her fingers toying with the dark curly hair on his chest. She drew back, looked into his blue eyes with her distant gaze and then scooted forward, straddling his hips, lifting herself, deftly lifting Shell's shaft, positioning him.

Her thighs trembled, her head was thrown back so that the tendons on her throat stood out tautly. Shell felt the heat of her body touch him, felt her slow settle, an inch at a time, felt the contact of her pelvis.

Sally sat erect, utterly still as if afraid to move. Then slowly she began to sway against him, to roll her hips from side to side, to thrust as Shell's hand found her buttocks and clenched the great trembling muscles there.

She gasped suddenly and fell against him, her fingers clawing at his shoulders, her mouth against his throat, his jaw, his lips as her body writhed spasmodically.

Shelter felt an answering demand in his loins and he arched his back as Sally reached back between her own legs to find Shell and claw at him. She cupped his sack, trying to draw him totally inside of her.

She was hot and damp and demanding. Her eager body smeared itself against Shell and as she cried out, sobbing, he buried himself to the hilt and finished with a draining, sudden climax.

Sally lay against him, her warm breath brushing Shell's throat, her hands still kneading his shoulder, kitten-like, her interior muscles still clenching and un-clenching as her breathing slowed, her pulse settled.

"I know you do like me," she said.

"Sure." Shell's palm moved across her back, down to the uptilt of her magnificent white buttocks and back to her neck. He felt the warm trickle of a tear running across his throat. Sally slowly sobbed in her fulfillment and Shelter clung to her.

Two of us, lonely in the night, he thought. Then he yawned and his hand halted its uncertain motion. When he awoke the room was dark and cold. Sally lay sleeping beside him, her hair in a yellow tangle.

The shadow loomed over him and Shelter knew what had awakened him. He saw the arm go up, but he was unable to react quickly enough and the club thudded down, catching him on the skull. Morgan went out in a starshower of brilliant lights. Voices called to him from the velvety depths and then there was nothing at all for a long while.

He opened his eyes to a gray dawn light. His head hammered with dull pain. One eye seemed not to want to focus. A brilliant white light kept winking on in his skull.

"Sally?"

He shook her shoulder. She still slept. Heavily. It was too heavily, Shelter realized, and when he looked at his hand he saw the smear of purplish blood on it.

"Sally!"

She didn't answer. She couldn't. There was a knife stuck into her back. Morgan's own bowie knife, and her mouth, open in some soundless exclamation would

41

never form any response again.

It was a time before Morgan, groggy and stunned, could make the decision to move. A little longer yet before he actually tried it. When he did sit up a heavy, clanging bell started ringing in his skull.

He slipped from the bed naked in the chill of morning. Everything was in place, the bureau apparently unrifled. His gunbelt still hung on the chair. And Sally's clothes still lay in a heap on the floor.

Shelter snatched up his pants and slipped them on, stamping into his boots. He stopped abruptly, spinning toward the door. There was someone clomping up the corridor, and he had a fair idea just who it would be.

He grabbed his shirt and gunbelt, and opening the window, stepped over the sill and out into the alley just as the door burst open behind him and Sheriff Colin Flowers, scattergun in hand, entered.

"There he goes!" someone shouted.

It was more a matter of there he went. Shelter took off at a dead run, racing for the corner of the alley. He just made it around as Flowers' ten-gauge cut loose, spraying the alley with double-ought buckshot.

Morgan never stopped. He raced for the stable as the sun dawned red behind him and Rembrandt came to slow life. A woman with a shopping basket over her arm swivelled her head as the half-dressed man rushed past her down the plankwalk.

"That way!" a voice from far behind yelled.

Morgan was already nearly to the stable. Another corner, fifty more feet and he was in through the door of the pole and mud building.

He should have known. Flowers was no fool and as

Shell rushed into the stable he knew he had made a mistake.

"Hands up, Morgan," the man behind him said.

Shell didn't even slow his motion. He leaped over the partition of the stable stall hearing the Winchester cut loose behind him. The .44-40 slug bored a hole in the partition, but Shell had kept moving. He wasn't about to get himself hung and Flowers had all he needed to do that little job. The citizens of Rembrandt wouldn't take kindly to the murder of a woman, even a saloon girl like Sally. And they wouldn't be listening to any argument that it was a frame-up.

Shell, on hands and knees scooted along the stable floor, the manure and rotten straw scent ripe in his nostrils. Ahead was a stack of loose hay and Shelter made for it.

He crawled to it, panting heavily, his eyes flickering back over his shoulder. He grabbed two huge handfuls of hay and cast them about the floor before darting in a crouch across the stall to where a wide-eyed gray horse stood watching him warily.

Shell got behind the horse and, grabbing the top of the partition pulled his feet up. There he hung, muscles taut, head hammering dully.

He heard the deputy padding across the stable floor, heard him stop, hesitate. Lifting his eyes an inch Shell saw the man stare at the hay, saw dull intelligence gleam in his eyes.

"Better come on out," the deputy said. He didn't say it twice. He lifted the rifle to his shoulder and fired three times into the haystack.

Shelter dropped silently to the floor and in three long, lunging steps was under the horse's belly and to the deputy. His Colt came up and then fell savagely, catching the deputy behind the ear. He caved in, sagging to the floor.

Shelter caught the Winchester as he fell. Turning away he grabbed the nearest saddle he saw and shouldered it. He found the sorrel two stalls down. The Mexican stablehand stood looking at him with anxious dark eyes. Back up the street there was lot of excited shouting going on.

"Open that back door," Morgan said sharply, and the hostler complied hurriedly.

Then Shelter was into leather, heeling the sorrel out into the daylight, lying low across the withers. A single distant shot rang out and then Shell was across the river and into the broken hills, Rembrandt vanishing from sight behind him.

4.

The low gray clouds nudged up against the red hills and the rain fell. Softly swirling, dreamlike it filled the valleys below Shelter Morgan and he looked skyward, thanking Providence.

They were still back there, had been all day. Sheriff Colin Flowers and his posse. By now they would be just a little weary, a little cold. The clouds blocked their vision and the rain worked away at the tracks the sorrel Morgan rode was leaving.

That was the good side of it. The trouble was, it wasn't half enough to balance the bad. There was a woman lying dead back there, and Shelter was the man they had made their minds up to hang.

He too was cold, his horse weary. He had no food, was in unknown country, with a posse behind him. If that wasn't enough he had company.

An hour earlier, crossing a sandy wash Shelter had seen the footprints. Apaches. They were in these hills as well, and they knew the country. All in all it was a rotten situation.

And he hadn't even heard a rumor concerning Able Sharpe.

Not a whisper. It was as if the man had dropped out of sight, never existed. Shell still couldn't convince himself that Benny Dierking had been mistaken. The man had been so sure.

"It was him," Dierking had whispered excitedly across the small round table in a Soccoro saloon. "I served under him, Morgan. The struttin' bastard. I know Able Sharpe, by God. I'd know him anywhere."

"Rembrandt, you say?"

"That's it. Rembrandt, Arizona. We were running freight up the Chiricahua Wells route. Me and Sampson Slade. Well, I was just pulling out of Rembrandt when I see him—Able Sharpe—riding in. I thought about pulling up, walking over and pressing five knuckles into his arrogant face, but I didn't. I didn't know then about them taking that gold and running out. The time I served with Sharpe was up in Carolina when we were with the 17th . . . anyway, I just didn't know about this other business. Tell you this," Benny winked, "I'll be happy to know that Sharpe got his. Maybe you could write me a note care of Western Freighting."

Shelter promised he would. Now it seemed he would never write that letter.

The storm lowered its head still more and Shelter hunched his shoulders against the wind, riding higher into the foothills.

He rode a crooked trail, keeping to stony surfaces when he could, doubling back frequently, taking the most unlikely routes. Still he had no confidence in his ability to escape the posse. He was a stranger in this

46

land, riding blind.

He was suddenly overlooking a wash where a white-water torrent surged downslope toward the flat desert beyond. Shell looked upstream and down, seeing no easy crossing anywhere. To get down to the freshet would mean sliding down a steep, clay-heavy bank. That might not be too difficult, but climbing the far bank would be. Still it had to be done. The very difficulty of it might slow the posse.

He eased the reluctant sorrel forward and over. The horse went nearly to its haunches, slid halfway down before finding its footing. It picked its way to the narrow ledge above the torrent at Shell's urging, but obviously felt misused by this new master.

Shell looked across the frothing creek, deciding against leaping for the far bank. It was too hazardous and he doubted the sorrel could scramble up the bank once over.

Instead he turned the horse left and walked it up the narrowing wash as the grey mist swirled down, the whitewater river foaming past.

The wash took a tight bend to Shell's left and he followed it. To come face to face with the lone Apache.

The man had been crouched under an overhanging ledge, keeping dry. The rain had muffled the sound of the approaching horse, and it had been altogether unexpected. The Apache was caught flat-footed.

His immobility didn't last long. He lunged for his nearby rifle and Shelter hurled himself from the sorrel after him. They collided roughly, Shell's body banging the Indian to the stony earth. They came up together, the Apache with a knife in hand.

Shell got a grip on the Apache's wrist and banged

away at his throat with his forearm. The first blow caught the windpipe and the Apache staggered back, gagging. Then he tucked in his chin and with mad fury twisted his knife hand free of Shell's tenacious grip.

Shell had to throw himself back to avoid the slashing knife. His back came up against the wall of the bluff behind him. He saw lightning crackle across the sky, felt the wind rush out of him, and he kicked out hard, keeping the Apache at a distance.

"Go on, get out of here!" Shell said, knowing that the man probably didn't understand him. He didn't want to fight, to kill or be killed. They had suddenly appeared in each other's path and now it seemed, for no reason but coincidence one must die on this stony wilderness ledge.

The Apache circled cautiously and Shell came out to meet him, his own bowie, the one which had been used to kill Sally, filling his hand. The Apache gave a little grunt as he saw the bared steel.

Shelter kept his left hand out, his right drawn back. He held the blade of the bowie up, ready to slash upward, to eviscerate. The Apache's eyes were black and cold. The wind up the gorge shrieked like a mad crone.

The Apache came in, cutting downward at Shell's wrist. Morgan parried and their knife blades clanged together. Shell kicked at the Indian's kneecap, trying to break it, but the blow was only a glancing one. The expression on the Apache's face didn't even change as the boot landed.

Shell backed away slowly, in a crouch, both hands out before him. The rock rolled under his feet and,

48

cursing, he felt his balance go. He saw the simultaneous flash of eagerness in his adversary's eyes, saw the Apache leap after him, blade poised.

Shelter hit the ground hard, rolled and twisted, narrowly avoiding the knife of the Apache. He managed to get a boot up and planted it solidly in the Indian's chest. The Apache was thrown back, landing clumsily.

Both men got to their feet again and they came together like two battling mountain sheep, their chests slapping together, eyes determined and narrow, every muscle taut and ready. Shelter was first to strike and his thrust was a deadly one. He felt the Indian writhe on his blade, felt the warm gush of blood onto his knife hand as he held the Indian against the bowie, digging upward to find the heart.

The Indian's own knife dropped free. His eyes were wide as he stared at Shelter, as he died on that cold ledge. Shelter withdrew his knife and the Apache slumped to the stone.

Panting, Morgan straightened up and wiped back his hair. He put his knife away, picked up his Colt and recovered the reins to the sorrel. Then, as another burst of lightning splintered the gray skies, he swung up and rode out along the wash.

He had gone a hundred yards when he heard the scream, and looking back he frowned, puzzled. Then he appeared. A second Apache standing atop the bluff, looking to where Shelter sat his horse.

The Indian snugged a rifle up to his shoulder, but Shell was off and riding up the twisting ravine before the bullet could reach him.

He rode swiftly over the broken trail, the rush of

water in his ears. He cursed himself bitterly. A second Apache—and how many more? Hundreds perhaps, and they would be on the trail of the white interloper. Yet there had been no choice about it and Morgan pushed the black thoughts from his mind, riding into the wind and rain.

He emerged from the gorge a mile on, surrounded by clouds. Looking back along his trail he could see nothing, but he was not deceived. The Apache would be coming. He had lost a brother, a friend, a tribesman. Only blood could satisfy him.

The clouds lifted as the afternoon wore on and darkness settled. Shelter made a camp atop a wind-swept knoll studded with nopal cactus. The sorrel chewed miserably at the dead dry grass as Morgan hunched against the red earth, staring out at his back trail.

Sunset was a purple flush across the red sand desert below. The hollows of the craggy broken hills were flooded with shadow. The wind-drifted clouds were touched with crimson and gold.

A distant mesa stood out in sharp relief, still lighted by the sun. Shelter Morgan leaned back and watched as it slowly darkened, like a waning candle.

He spent the night that way, watching, listening, his rifle across his knees. He wanted more than anything else to sleep, to close his raw red eyes for one moment, but he didn't dare.

They were back there, all the hunters, and they would be coming.

He rose stiffly in the morning, watching the desert emerge from the night shadows. He saddled the sorrel and stood looking out across the hills. Which way? East was Rembrandt and the necktie party, west the

Apache stronghold. To the south was Mexico, but it was a long trek across bad country, and he didn't feel he could make it had he wanted to.

And he didn't. He wanted Able Sharpe.

He wondered—had it been Sharpe who framed him? It seemed it had to be. Who else in Rembrandt would have reason? Somehow Sharpe must have discovered his presence and set Morgan up. And Sally had been the one to pay the price.

Shelter's jaw set as he stood leaning against the sorrel's flank, thinking on that. It had to have been Sharpe, damnit! That meant the man was nearby, possibly living in Rembrandt. And he had friends to carry the word that Morgan was in town. Friends to deny his existence.

All of that speculation did Shell no immediate good. He stepped into leather and headed off down the slope of the hill, riding north blindly.

The hills which had been barren now began to be dusted with scattered scrub cedar, and here and there with deprived pinyon pines. There was oak and willow in the bottoms where the water from yesterday's rain still rushed toward the desert flats below where it would be swallowed up in a matter of days, leaving the country dry and desolate once again.

Shell halted his sorrel on a saddleback ridge. Smoke. He saw smoke rising, pencil thin, gray against the deep blue of the sky, not four miles off.

It could have been an Indian's fire, the campfire of the posse. It could have been almost anything, but Shell was determined to have a look-see. The horse was worn out, he himself was weary and hungry. He had to have food, water and feed for the horse. He

51

started off down the canyon, ducking low to clear a wind-twisted cedar which hung out across the trail.

The wind was brisk up the canyon. Four hundred feet below the creek rushed past. A blue jay squawked at Morgan from the manzanita brush. And the rifle shot echoed down the canyon as the searing pain tore at Morgan's chest.

He clasped hands to his chest, felt the sorrel rear and throw him, felt himself hit the ground hard and begin to roll, the rifle shot still echoing in his head, the incredible pain like molten metal poured over his chest.

Then he bounced off a huge red boulder and he felt no more, heard no more.

It seemed hours later when he forced his eyes open, some deep instinct for survival prodding him to consciousness, and he saw the dark face of the Apache above him, saw the rifle in his hand, the red headband he wore, the savage scar scrolled across his copper cheek.

Then the second shot came and Shelter saw the Indian buck, sprawl lifeless to the earth. Then for a while Morgan saw no more.

"Are you all right?"

The voice penetrated his fuzzy mind, nudging a grunting response from Shelter. He opened one eye then although even that seemed to cause pain.

"Yes. I'm all right."

"Sure. So I was right about you, was I? You came following me anyway."

"What?"

"Who are you working for, Mister Morgan?"

"Who?"

"Hell. Never mind. Right now I've got to get you patched up," Coral Scant said. She put her rifle aside, but within reach and crouched over him, sucking at her lower lip intently as she opened Shell's shirt and examined the wound. "You got the luck, Mister Morgan."

"Yeah, it feels like it."

"Another inch and it wouldn't have felt like anything," Coral answered. The bullet had gone across Shell's chest, digging a groove through the meat. The blood was copious, the pain intense, but it was not a dangerous wound unless infection set in.

"You hold on a minute."

"Think I'm going to run out?" Shelter cracked.

Coral didn't answer. She was digging through the saddlebags hung over the flanks of a patient old jenny mule. She returned with her hands full.

"Know what you're doing?" Shell asked.

"I'd better," she said and Morgan laughed. It hurt, but he laughed.

"Easy now, you bastard," Coral said. "Here." She gave him a metal flask which Shell fumbled with but could not open. His hands seemed three times their normal size. Swollen, useless. Coral kept jumping in and out of focus, although when she was in focus, she was a sight worth looking on.

He studied the serious, puckered lips, the long-lashed dark eyes, the small round ears. She wore a flop hat, a buckskin riding skirt and a white blouse. Beneath it her breasts made appealing points of interest.

"Here."

She had opened the flask and she supported Shell's head while he drank deeply of the brandy. His nostrils, his lungs caught fire as the alcohol worked its magic. Coral watched him, her rigidity seeming to fade to more tender emotion for a single moment.

"You'll want more," she said, regaining her stiffness. She folded his hand around the flask.

She squatted on her heels concentrating as she threaded a needle. "That for me?" Shelter asked.

"If you could see your chest you wouldn't have to ask," she said snappishly. "I ought to let you bleed to death for following me up here, but I guess I owe you something for the stagecoach."

"Look, Coral . . ."

"Be quiet, Morgan! Take another drink. This is going to hurt."

It did. Like hell. Shelter was grateful for the liquor. Coral cleaned the wound and then began sewing the flaps of flesh together, working with deep concentration, breathing tightly through her mouth which was pursed, dry.

She was still working when Shelter passed out.

When he came to he was in the same position. But the sun had risen higher and now glared directly down into his eyes. Coral was dusting him with flour to aid the coagulation. There was a smudge of flour on her forehead, a spot of Shell's blood on her white blouse.

"You're going to live, I expect," she said, and Shelter smiled, liking the girlish menace in her voice. She flushed with exasperation and stood, looking down at him, hands on hips. A wisp of dark hair blew across her forehead and Shell watched it for a long while. He must have passed out again because he was suddenly aware of being upright, leaning against the jenny mule. Coral was panting with exertion.

54

"You lift me up?"

"I did," she said fiercely. "You were no help."

"You're very pretty," Shelter said, touching her nose. His voice seemed oddly slurred, his tongue thick. It was amusing—but not to Coral.

"Just step back, Mister Morgan. This is no picnic."

"No." Somehow he had gotten up on the mule, and he looked down at Coral who wavered before his vision. "Where now?"

"Now, damn you, you're going to get your wish. I'll have to take you along home with me."

That made no sense to Shelter—his wish? He had no wish at all but that the pain would go away, the brandy clear off. Oh, and it might have been nice to lean over and kiss her little pink ear, but he would fall off the mule if he tried that and he knew it.

"Whatever you say," he replied. "Anywhere you're going."

Coral looked at him with infinite disgust and turned, leading the mule down the steep canyon. Shelter sat on the mule's back, singing a merry little song in what seemed to him to be fine voice until he fell off the jenny and rapped his head and the lights went out.

5.

When Shelter next opened his eyes it was dark. A candle was burning somewhere not far away. He could see the faint glow, smell the tallow. And his head was throbbing like Satan's misery.

There were hundreds of little men in there playing an anvil chorus. He lay his head back on the pillow, wondering where a pillow could have come from out on this desert. Thinking about it hurt his head and he gave it up, trying to think of nothing, to remember nothing.

He had closed his eyes, but they flickered open now. He had smelled the candle burning and now that smell was nearer. Peering through nearly closed eyelids he saw the candle, its flame a red spear point. And behind the candle a lovely, dark haired girl in a white night dress. Her hair was loose and long around her shoulders. He could see the contours of her breasts through the material of her gown. Her eyes were dark, round and wide.

"Ah," he said, his hand lifting, and the expression on the girl's face changed from concerened innocence to precocious cynicism.

"Awake. I thought so," she said.

"Alive."

"Hurt?"

"It hurts, yes. Don't I know you?" Shell asked from out of his confusion.

"No."

"I must. Sit down here."

"Like hell. You're playing possum on me, Morgan."

"Coral Scant," he said as it came back to him.

"Coral Scant, that's right. I guess you succeeded after all, Mister Morgan."

"Did I?" Shell looked her up and down. Had he bedded her, crawled all over her lovely young body? She was flushing now behind the candle.

"That's not what I meant," she said. "God, what a mind you've got."

"Where did I succeed? Sorry, it's a little fuzzy upstairs."

"You're here, aren't you?" Coral snapped. Then she turned and walked away, out of the dark, windowless room and Morgan lay there staring after the diminishing light. He had succeeded. In what he did not know, could not recall. But he was with her, although she seemed to be miffed. He was safe in her bed and that was enough for now, enough success for this night.

When she came again she was dressed in a man's flannel shirt of an off-red color, blue jeans, boots and wide brimmed hat. It was morning, or should have been, yet Coral carried a candle. There was no sunlight seeping into this room, no light anywhere but from the wick of Coral's candle.

57

"Are you feeling all right?" she asked dryly.

"Yes."

"Good. Last night you were out of your head. You remember it?" she asked.

"Vaguely. Had a dream that a pretty young thing came to see me wearing a nightgown."

"Still out of your head," Coral said. "Throw down that blanket. Let me have a look at your chest."

Shell complied, and Coral, placing the candle holder on a crude bedside table which appeared to be made of an apple crate, untied the dressing across Shell's chest.

"Easy," he said as the scab tore free. "Kind of rough aren't you?"

"You deserve more?"

"I don't know. What exactly have I done to you, Coral Scant? I know my mind has been playing tricks on me with the brandy you fed me and the loss of blood, but I don't recall what in hell it is I might have done to get you so damned mad at me, girl."

"All innocence, aren't you?"

"Can't claim that," he admitted.

"No, I guess not." She fingered the wound which was puckered and pink. Healing, but not quickly. "You'll be down a few more days."

"Coral—I can't stay down long," Shelter said, taking her wrist in his hand. She started to pull away but gave in. She frowned at him questioningly.

"Why not? Oh, I see, you've got to get back to them."

"What? Do we understand each other? Everything we say seems at cross-purposes. I'm going to make you a bargain, Coral Scant. I'll tell you exactly what I'm talking about, and then you tell me exactly what you think I'm doing. What all this is about. Is it a deal?"

"Maybe." Coral tried again to pull her wrist free but Shelter held her even more tightly. "Right now I don't seem to have a choice. "Tell me what it is that's on your mind," she sighed.

"It's this way," Shell began, and he told her the whole long bloody story, taking it all the way back to Georgia, to the Conasauga. "When I finally did get to Rembrandt no one had ever heard of Able Sharpe, but someone knew something. Someone got word to the man. There was a woman I met in town. A good woman, I think. Not the cleverest in the world, but a good-hearted girl. Someone killed her, Coral, someone stabbed her with my knife and left it to the law to dispose of me.

"I made my break and hit these hills. What you're doing here, what your secrets may be, I don't know. It doesn't matter a lot to me. I want one thing—to find Able Sharpe before the law finds me."

Coral listened thoughtfully, her dark eyes growing wider yet, her face paling. Finally she asked, "Who was the woman?"

Shelter laughed out loud and Coral's face suffused with blood. "What's so darned funny!"

"Nothing, Coral, nothing at all. It just seemed to be a woman's question. Only a woman would ask first 'Who was she?' "

"Is that so?" Coral demanded, wrenching her wrist free. "Well maybe, just maybe someone would be concerned enough to want to know who had been killed!"

Shelter turned suddenly, deeply serious. "You're right, Coral. Right to feel the way you do. Don't think for a minute I've forgotten about this woman, about the way she died. They marked her out as if her existence was meaningless. Just a tool for their use. Well, I won't forget, and the bastard that did it will pay for it, believe me. She had worth."

Coral was silent. She sat on the bed beside Shelter, thoughtful and serious. "I don't want to know her name," she said quietly. "Really I don't." Shell's hand covered hers and Coral flinched before smiling weakly and shrugging.

"Now you," Shelter said.

"What?"

"We had a bargain. I told you my story, told you what I was doing in these hills. Now suppose you tell me exactly what it is you're up to, what your secret is."

"I can't."

"All right." Shell gripped her hand, winked and smiled.

"If I could . . ."

"I said it was all right, Coral. It doesn't matter. It's just that I thought maybe you needed some help."

Suddenly she snapped. Tears began to trickle out of her eyes, and she didn't look tough, resilient any more, just small, feminine and very young.

"I do need help! There's no one, absolutely no one I can trust. You understand that!"

"Sure."

"I didn't mean you."

"Why should you trust me? You're not going to hurt my feelings very easily, Coral. I know what I look like, what I sound like—I wouldn't trust me either, and if you don't want to, well, that's fine enough. I'll lay here and heal and be on my way."

"But you don't understand, I do want to trust you.

It's just that . . . There's gold," she said, taking sudden resolution. She spoke to him distantly, looking at the wall and not at Shelter's face.

"Gold," he said evenly. "Someone else wants it."

"Yes." She whirled to face him, her eyes intent. "My father was a prospector, working these hills, others like them for thirty years. Thirty years, Morgan! And I was with him for the last twenty of those. Do you know what kind of life that was for him? Working till his body ached, the hardest kind of labor. His eyes—I could see it there. The anguish as I grew older, as he began to feel he had let me down that he would have nothing to leave me, that I would never have a chance at an education, an opportunity to wear decent clothes."

Shelter understood too well. It happened, and it was a far from uncommon thing. A man working to do for his children watching as the dreams slipped away, feeling futile, not knowing that the gift of love was all that counted with the kids.

Shelter noticed that Coral had not said a thing about her own privations. It must have been difficult for her. Never going to socials with young men, never having new dresses. Living in these empty hills with the Indians around them, the old man killing himself in a hole in the ground.

"He finally hit it," Coral said, deciding to go all the way with her story. "A regular mother lode, Morgan—oh, it's not the Comstock, but for a one-man mine it was truly amazing, a bonanza. A glittering dream."

"Indian?" Shell guessed.

"No. The Apaches had come to respect Father, I think. In their way. It was a white man who killed

61

. . . who killed him. Just as he was on the verge of seeing it all come true."

"You were here?"

"I was," Coral said. "I buried him out here. Then I walked to the shaft and caved it in. I started a landslide up on the hill and buried the mine. I turned then and walked away from it. I didn't want it. I had only wanted . . . my father."

"They didn't ever find the mine?" Shelter asked.

"No. These hills are peppered with old shafts. Most of them Father dug. They could spend as many years as he did searching for it. And then there's the Apaches. Oh, I imagine they came looking but they never found it. I thought—it seemed that you might be following me up here to find out where it is."

"What happened, Coral? Why did you come back?"

"At first I couldn't stand to be here anymore. Not without Father. I went to Indiana to stay with my aunt. I went to school, got a little education. I owed that to Father, Shell. He always wanted it."

Shelter nodded, but Coral didn't seem to notice him. She looked into the candlelight, her fingers clasped.

"I got to thinking about what else I owed him. I don't want that gold, Shelter, I never did. But *he* did. He wanted me to have it. Too, he wanted the world to know he wasn't a fool, wasn't that 'crazy Aaron Scant.' When I finished school I worked for a while dated a few men, but there was something wrong. Something left undone, something haunting me.

"In the middle of the night I woke up in a sweat. It came back to me suddenly. It was the mine. Maybe I'm superstitious, but it seemed that Father was calling to me out of his grave, asking me to come back and show them all!" Coral smiled with embarrassment.

"But there's a risk. Folks around here would know why you came back."

"Yes, and when the stagecoach was hit, I'm sure it was me they wanted. I think they know I'm back somehow."

"But you're not sure, and you didn't want me telling the sheriff that you were on that stage."

"No. It would send them crawling over these hills, Shell. All right—someone knows, but the fewer the better. I don't want it to become general knowledge."

"But you have a legal claim," Shell said.

"Yes. You know what that's worth out here. If they find it, if they want it, they'll take it."

"Who?" Shell asked and Coral almost looked startled. She frowned at him in puzzlement. "Who will take it, Coral? Who is it you're up against?"

"I don't know," she said, waving a hand in a vague gesture. "I never knew who killed Father. The sheriff said he tried to find out, but I didn't see much evidence of that. I just don't know. I can think of a dozen men who would do it without compunctions."

"And the town itself—would the folks stand for it?"

"I don't know." Coral ran a hand through her dark hair. "If the gold began to come in, maybe they would. Haven't you seen Rembrandt? It's a dying town. There used to be a little mining along the creek, some timber cutting east of town. Now the timber's gone, the creek panned dry. The only thing keeping Rembrandt alive is the cow outfits up north. Those people have to spend their money somewhere. Maybe they wouldn't object so much to new money coming into town."

"Is the operation going to be that large?" Shell asked.

"Large enough to employ men? To keep freight wagons running, ore wagons, a smelter, yes. Or, I should say it could be."

"Seems like the town would want to protect you then, Coral Scant. Maybe you're just what those people have been waiting for. A goose that lays golden eggs."

Coral shook her head. "Maybe. Maybe so. All I do know is that I'm going to work that mine. I'm going to open the shaft up again and prove that Aaron Scant wasn't crazy, that his daughter isn't either. To hell with the Apaches and with Rembrandt and my father's killers!"

And Shelter smiled. She was quite a girl this one. Tough beneath the pretty surface, confident, courageous. But he knew too well that courage didn't win battles. He had seen that proven long ago in his War. Then it had been guns, numbers that won, not raw courage.

In the candlelight Coral Scant looked small, too young, weary, and despite her brave talk, she was frightened. Shell could see it deep in her eyes. Well, he decided, she had the right to be scared. He made one other decision. He was going to hang around for a while. The girl needed help and she was going to get none anywhere else.

It wasn't the promise of glittering gold that decided Shell, it was the softer glowing of those dark eyes as the candle burned low and Coral Scant took his hand between her own soft hands and smiled again, trying to be brave before she fell against him, her shoulders trembling as she sobbed against his chest.

6.

It was two days before Shelter got up from his bed and dressed slowly, carefully, not wanting to split open the chest wound. Coral came upon him as he was tugging on his boots and she stood in the doorway, hands on hips, watching him.

"About time," she said finally.

Shelter noticed the rock dust on her clothing, the gloves on her hands, the severely knotted back hair. She had been hard at work somewhere. Strangely the dishevelment, the work clothes made her especially appealing on this morning. He looked her up and down, liking the way the man's jeans clung to her hips and thighs.

"Oh, no," Coral said. "Don't tell me I've been nursing a wolf here."

"Maybe."

"Well, draw in your fangs, Shelter Morgan. I'm here to work, and if you stay, that's what you're here for too. Though I don't see how you're going to do much for a while."

"I'll manage," he assured her.

"Maybe you will. You seem to be a determined sort of a man."

"When I go after what I want." He had stepped nearer to her now, towering over her and Coral's lips compressed in disdain.

"I told you about that already," she said, placing her hands on Shell's chest, shoving him away. He winced and she realized she had touched his still tender wound. "Well," Coral said, "you deserved that anyway."

"You're probably right. All right. It's all business between us. Suppose you show me a little of what we're doing?"

"Up to a little climb?"

"If I have to be."

"You have to be. In case your nimble mind hasn't deduced it yet, this room you're standing in is underground."

Shell's nimble mind had deduced that. Even at midday the room was never warm. At night the temperature didn't drop much. There were no windows in the "cabin," no light but that of the candles.

"Father built it down here—in the cavern—as protection against the heat. In the summer it's killing to be out in the sun. Down here it was always cool, dark." She looked around the room, remembering other times.

"And safe from the Apaches?" Shelter asked.

"That's it. They never did find us, nor did any of the prowlers."

"Prowlers?"

"Claim-jumpers, nosy Parkers. Come on, I'll show you the way up."

The cavern was small, globular. Water trickling downward had carved it out of the limestone over the eons. In all it was no more than a hundred feet square. Above Shell saw a pinprick of light reached by a long, shaky-appearing ladder.

"When the ladder's taken away a man would break his leg at the least trying to get down here."

At the least. It was thirty feet up to the top where a brushy mat of gray native material covered the entrance to the pit.

Shelter could feel the heat wafting down as they neared the surface, and as Coral pushed the brushy screen aside and they clambered up into the glaring sunlight, his body reeled as a wave of dry heat hit him full force.

"Nice spring day," Coral said. "Now you see why Father built our place down below."

"How in hell did you get me down there?" Shell wanted to know.

"With a rope around your arms and my jenny mule lowering," Coral said. "Come along now, the day's a-wastin'."

They walked up a flame-colored arroyo to a yawning, shallow cave where the jenny mule, straw trickling from its lips was kept out of the sun. Shelter's sorrel was there as well, looking fit again.

"Where are we going?" Shell asked as they saddled.

"Right up to the mine," Coral replied. "No sense fooling around now."

"I don't mind a little fooling around," Shelter said across the sorrel's back. Coral didn't answer. She was looking at the flank of Shelter's mount.

"Rafter CB," she said, reading the brand.

"That's right," Morgan answered. "Do you know it?"

"Of course. Carl Brunner. Everyone around here knows that brand."

"Not everyone," Shell told her. "The sheriff didn't recognize it."

"Oh, but he must have," Coral said, her eyes narrowing as she looked from the brand to Shell's eyes.

"Well, if he knew, he didn't admit it to me."

"Maybe he didn't want you going off half-cocked."

"Maybe."

"After all, just because the horse that outlaw was riding carried Rafter CB's brand, it doesn't follow that Carl Brunner is involved."

"No."

"He sells hundreds of horses."

"Sure." It seemed that Coral was defending this man to Shell. Or maybe to herself. "Do you know him?"

"Well, I used to. Yes. He was one of the few people around here who was ever friendly with Father. He loaned us money once or twice," she said, looking down at the ground sheepishly. "When things were so tough we didn't have a can of beans. He runs a ranch thirty miles north of here along the Carrizo. Mostly horses, but a few hundred head of shorthorns. He has a nice house of the kind you don't see much around here. White frame, two stories."

"Sounds like money."

"Oh he's well enough off, but he's not the money-hungry sort. No—don't start suspecting Carl Brunner. He sells many horses to all sorts of men. He doesn't go around robbing stagecoaches. He's fine, noble, proud . . ."

"Good-looking?" Shell asked devilishly and he saw Coral flush to the tips of her ears.

"He's too old for me," she managed to say, but still her expression was crowded with embarrassment. She stepped into her stirrups and swung a leg over the jenny mule's back, settling into the saddle. "You ready, Mister Morgan?"

"Ready," he said, still grinning. He walked the sorrel out behind Coral's mule and together they headed west, up the jagged sloping canyon where boulders stood in reddish clusters against soil-less, eroded hillsides.

Shell began to see signs of workings here and there. Small craters, test shafts pecked here and there across the landscape. Rockslides, the litter of flash floods stood everywhere. Any of them might have been caused by nature or man. Shelter began to understand why no one could have found this mine without Coral's help.

He watched her sitting that jenny mule, back erect, rifle across the mule's withers. And she could use that rifle! It had been a timely, dead shot which took that Apache down as he loomed over Shell.

"Up here," she said, and Morgan looked up a raw, scorched slope toward a crumbled mesa-like highland. There was volcanic rock scattered everywhere like blackened petrified sponges; they were porous and smooth. Nothing but yucca grew on the slope, yet as they crested the highland, their mounts laboring, Shelter found himself looking at grassland and cedars.

The grass was pale green, and the cedars bedraggled. The wind was hot, flowing across the caprock, but still it was a sudden, unexpected vista.

"Water seeps up from somewhere below," Coral said. "It's artesian, I suppose, since wherever it pools it's very cold as if it had come up from far down."

They crossed the grasslands and came to a canyon which fell away sharply toward the red sand desert beyond. Looking southward Shell could see Mexico, a mirage lake spreading across the flats, an endless white playa. Nothing but raw untamed land.

"Down there," Coral said, indicating the canyon which looked as if man had never walked it. The earth was yellow-gray, boulders strewn everywhere. There appeared to be no sort of trail, track or game path.

"Rough to get ore up out of there," Shell said.

"Father's idea was to take it down to the desert floor then around, back up the Carrizo and into Rembrandt," Coral answered.

"That might be all right with wagons and teams, men and equipment, but it's a hell of a job for the two of us."

"I know that. We just need a start, Shelter. A little ore will get us a team, a little more, a wagon."

"And at that first little sign of ore everyone will know you're up here." Shell stepped down to stand looking at the slope-sided canyon. Coral, holding the reins to her mule stood beside him, a head shorter, much smaller.

"Yes. They'll know."

"You said you didn't care about the gold," Morgan said, turning her by the shoulders. "Maybe you were right. This is wild country and you're going to be easy prey. The claim is open to any man with a gun. Once you start showing that ore, they'll be coming."

"What are you saying? Give up?"

"I'm just reminding you how it will be. That it's going to be dangerous."

"You can pull out whenever you want to," she said, her words clipped and salty.

Shell looked down the canyon, then back to the small dark-eyed girl. He winked, "Show me what you've got down there, Coral Scant."

They descended part way on horseback, but two hundred feet along the trail became impossibly steep and they had to leave the jenny and the sorrel on a small, sheltered ledge to pick at the dry forage while they continued on foot.

Ten minutes of that and Shell began to wish he had stayed in bed. His head began to ache as the hot sun glared off the boulders and into his eyes. The chest wound stung as sweat dripped into it. His stamina was shot from the blood he had lost.

"Well," Coral said, "better sit down. No sense killing yourself, is there?"

"How much farther is it?" Shell asked.

"A quarter of a mile."

"I think I'll sit. No sense killing myself."

She smiled and Shell, placing his butt on a long, smooth rock threw back his head and breathed in deeply, slowly. And this was where she was going to try to freight ore! The canyon continued downward another mile, the sloping floor gradually giving way to sand which drifted in off the flats. The going through that sand would be nearly as difficult as climbing up out of the canyon. Not considering the Apaches it was a hell of a task. With them—well, it didn't look good with any force less than an army to Morgan.

"Hope you've got some ore down there worth this," Shell said, trying not to let his deep concern show.

"Wait until you've seen it, Morgan," she said with a

71

wink. "You'll find out that it's worth it. I know this is bad country, but it'll work. It has to," she said, her eyes lifting to the far horizon as the dry wind gusting up the canyon toyed with her dark hair.

"Well, let's see." Shell rose, nodded, and they continued on down, picking their way through boulders as high as a cottage, great pale monoliths that had been standing through the centuries while wind and rain scrubbed away the soil which had once surrounded them.

Shell began to see more quartz now, and looking at the shelf of buckled granite above and beyond him, he began to admit to himself that it looked like gold country. But how much? As he had told Coral a small amount—a few thousand dollars worth—would not be worth the working. The ore would have to be carried up in gunny sacks, taken to Rembrandt or some other shipping point, freighted to someplace where there was an ore-crusher and smelter. All of that would consume the profit before it was refined. Likely it would be a losing proposition. Coral, however, looked confident, and he hoped for her sake that she was right, that her father's dream, her dream was more than that, that it was reality and not some resurrected fantasy over which Coral would waste her own life.

"Here we are," she said, stopping suddenly. The ground around them was over-tracked by Coral's small bootprints. She had been doing some work here, but there was a ton of it left to do.

The boulders lay scattered everywhere, stacked like a stony sepulcher in a dry, deep wash.

"When you caved it in, you did a job, didn't you?"

"I couldn't take a chance on anyone finding the shaft."

"Where is it?" he asked, wiping his forehead with his sleeve.

Coral looked at him a minute longer, deciding again if she could trust this tall, lean stranger. Finally she nodded. "Come along, I'll show you."

She led him upslope to where someone—Coral—had obviously been clearing away stone. She had used lever and fulcrum, her mule apparently, though how she had gotten it down here Shelter couldn't guess, and plenty of muscle. What she had done was no more than a gesture. If there was a shaft under that stone no part of it was visible yet.

"Inside it will be caved in too, won't it?"

"Probably. But Father timbered heavily and the earth around the shaft was very solid." Coral must have noticed the skeptical expression on Shell's face. "It's not so bad as it looks," she said with a brave smile. "Come here, I'll show you."

She led Shell to a hollow between rocks. A massive flat boulder formed a roof over two opoosing stacks of yellow rocks. Coral walked straight in, Shelter ducking slightly. Fifteen feet back Coral paused, picked up a lantern from the ground where tools also lay. She lit the lantern, replaced the chimney and nodded.

By the lanternlight Shell saw the massive, tilted timbering. The slide had done its damage but the header above what had once been a shaft entrance was still in place.

"That's it," she said, almost reverently.

Shell could see where she had dragged some rock out of the mouth of the shaft. Again he studied the timbers. The uprights had sagged forward beneath the header, but they still seemed to be taking the load and

73

appeared to be solid, unsplintered.

"I'd hate to be the first one in there," Shell said.

"Well, you won't be!" Coral said with some anger. "I'll be the first."

"All right," Shell smiled, "settle now, woman. It was just an observation."

His voice echoed dully off the stone around him. Coral shrugged an apology and motioned to Shell. He crouched as she lowered the lantern and the light gleamed dully on the rocks at her feet. There it was. Thin streaks of gold, and damned pure stuff, nearly jewelry grade gleamed in the few dozen small samples at Coral's feet.

"This is some of the rock Father brought up from below. He was going to have it assayed, but he never . . . you can see can't you? Have you ever done any mining?"

"Some," Shelter replied, preferring not to think about his mining career which had been an enforced one. He had done some slave labor work, long ago. "I know what this is." He picked up a small sample and turned it over in his hands. "Is this typical, you think?"

"I've no idea. If it is?"

"If it is, you'll be able to justify all of this work. Yes," Shelter rose, dusting his hands together. "If the other ore even approaches this high grade stuff, it would be worth any trouble and expense to bring it up."

"Now," Coral said, her head cocked to one side, "isn't that exactly what I told you, Mister Morgan?"

And Shelter gathered her into his arms, kissing her deeply. She gasped with surprise. For a moment her body was rigid, protesting, her lips dry and set, but then she warmed. Her knees buckled and it seemed

74

that if Shelter let go, she would sag to the earth. Her lips parted and she met his kiss warmly, briefly. Then she recovered herself.

"Sure—now that you find out I'm a rich girl," she joked, pushing away from him. But there was more than amusement in her eyes. Some deep fire had been kindled and they both knew it. "There's nothing else to be done here today," Coral said, picking up the lantern hastily. "You're in no condition for it."

"Try me."

"The digging, I meant, Shelter Morgan."

"What did you think I meant?" he asked, crowding close to her so that her breasts were only inches from his chest. She seemed to hold her breath, afraid of rubbing up against him at this moment, in this place.

"Come on," she said with mock savagery. Then she ducked and was under his arm and away. Shelter turned, grinning, to follow her out into the piercing daylight.

Getting back up the slope was a labor in itself. Shelter had to admit Coral was right about one thing—he was hardly ready to be of any help working that mine.

By the time they had reached the ledge where the sorrel and the jenny mule were picketed, Shell was done in. He sat down, his back against the rising bluff behind him and took in deep gulps of air as the blood coursed through his veins, his head throbbed.

In minutes it was throbbing still more, the blood racing even more quickly.

Coral, standing over him, nodded her head as with decision and slowly began unbuttoning her blouse.

7.

Shelter watched, his exhausted body finding new life, his loins stirring as Coral Scant, humming softly to herself removed her blouse and smiled down at Shelter Morgan. She ran her hands up across her small, firm breasts.

"Like them?"

"What do you think?"

"I think you do," she said. She bent low and kissed Shell's forehead, her breasts swinging tantalizingly inches from his lips as she rose, stepped back and began working at the buttons of her jeans.

There was almost no breeze on the stony ledge where Shell sat, his weary body coming to life. The rock beneath him, behind him was sun-warm still although the sun was dropping rapidly toward the horizon, the desert flushing to deep red.

Coral Scant stepped from her jeans, standing before Morgan in some brief underthing that reached to mid-thigh. Then, still smiling, she slid that down over her sleek young hips and stood before him in boots, the sundown skies casting tinted reflections against her flesh.

She walked to him and stood over him, and Shelter ran his hands up her thighs, his thumbs joining at the downy junction of her legs, finding soft, warm flesh beneath the dark thicket.

Coral seemed hardly aware of his presence. She stood looking upward, her hands still on her hips, her head thrown back, eyes distant as Shell softly probed her damp recess. She seemed hardly aware, but her thighs began to tremble as Shell's roving fingers dipped inside of her, as his lips touched the hollow of her thigh inches below her pelvis and she sagged suddenly into his arms, tearing his shirt open as she collapsed against him, her hands groping at his crotch, finding the growing erection there.

In another minute she had his pants off, tugging at the cuffs, her eyes on his crotch as he sprang free. Shell was afraid she was going to lose her balance and fall over the lip of the ledge. She was a woman who knew what she wanted now, and was going to have it.

Excitement fired her eyes as Shell rose, and she walked to him, cool small hands encircling his shaft, her breasts pressed against his chest.

She bent low, her warm kisses stitching patterns across her abdomen as her fingers manipulated Shell. Then she was against him, her belly to his, her face contorted with pleasure, with anticipation as she lifted one leg, and standing on tiptoes managed to get the head of Shelter's shaft positioned inside the soft, inviting envelope of her flesh.

She was heedless of his wound now, as was Shell. She wrapped her arms around his neck and hoisted herself, her body quivering as she clamped herself around Morgan, her feet interlocking behind his waist, her pelvis slowly settling as she took him into her moist, needful body.

The sun was a dying rose, a crimson mist above a distant mesa. Coral, her legs wrapped around him was a surging warmth, a nymph, a primal urge as old as the desert as she slid against him, her eyes blank with passion, her body electric with need.

She gripped his buttocks as Shell held her shoulders, his back arching, his own rhythm building steadily toward a climax. Her finger dipped down into the crack of his ass, and she shuddered as he worked against her, burying himself to the hilt.

She lifted a breast to his lips, squeezing her own nipple until it must have hurt until Shell's lips took it in, his tongue running in whorls around the taut, sensitive flesh.

Coral murmured something which made no sense outside of her world of sensuality, of need, and as her body seemed to ripen, to split wide, and Shell felt a fluid rush, a clenching of her inner muscles, his own loins were racked with release and he filled her violently, sagging to the rock, Coral with him, perched on top of his driving body. Her hands tore at her own breasts as she straddled him. Her mouth was open wide in a silent shriek.

"Now, now . . ." she murmured and Shelter felt her slip from him. She rolled over and was on hands and knees, spreading herself, showing her deep pink conduit to him, and he eased up behind her as grappling hands found him.

She fingered herself, inching Shelter inside of her

78

simultaneously, shaking and pitching against him until she collapsed onto her face, Shell following her down, his hands reaching under her to grip her breasts as if they would squeeze warm milk from them and she moaned with the pain or with the pleasure reaching yet another climax as Shell buried himself in her, his pelvis slamming against her milky buttocks, throbbing in the sweet crevice until he came again, sharply and fell against her, still pulsing, still satisfying Coral Scant.

It was dark by the time they clambered up out of the canyon, the well-rested animals pointed homeward. Homeward—toward a dugout hole in the ground. It was dark, the cedars only stark, grasping silhouettes against the sky, but not dark enough to hold back the sniper's twitching finger.

The shot racketed across the highlands and Shelter threw himself from the horse's back, grabbing at the shrieking Coral Scant.

They hit the ground hard as the sorrel danced away in fright.

"Are you hurt! Are you hurt!" Coral shouted.

"Quiet!" Shell's hiss was commanding. He clamped his hand over her mouth and she nodded.

"I thought you'd been shot," she whispered into his ear. Her hand gripped his arm tightly.

Shell paid little attention to Coral. His eyes searched the darkness. The cool Colt revolver filled his hand. He hadn't been shot, but it was a near thing. The sniper was good, whoever he was.

He had been hurt, however. The jolt of throwing himself to the ground had ripped open flesh and muscle on his chest and now he was fighting back the waves of nausea and pain which swept over him.

"Come on. Silently," he whispered into Coral's ear. He dragged her back along the earth toward a small damp depression fifty feet behind him. They slid backward into it, Shell's Colt cocked, waiting the second shot from the sniper's rifle, his eyes searching for the muzzle flash, his ears intently alert for any sound.

He heard nothing, saw nothing.

"Stay here," he ordered Coral.

"Where are you going!" she whispered frantically, squeezing his arm until it hurt. There was panic in her eyes.

"Hunting," he said. "Now stay and be quiet."

It was time again. Time for the battle. Man meeting man in a struggle for life. Another battlefield, another war. Shelter sucked it up, drew his legs under him and prepared to move out.

There was no way he was going to allow the sniper to sit out there waiting for a clear shot. He would have them pinned down all night, and the slightest mistake on their part could lead to bloody death for Shelter—or for Coral.

He would take it to him. Shelter had never minded facing death. He had lived in the face of it. What he minded was the helpless feeling which comes upon a man surrounded by the threat of death who has no way at all of fighting back, of announcing his own determination to survive.

He began to move, slipping down the depression, away from the sniper. He went an eighth of a mile before he began his slow return movement. He kept to the shadows, his eyes hurting with the effort to pierce the darkness, to see through the deep shadows cast by the cedars.

The sniper might have cleared out by now. It was likely, but Shelter hoped he had not. The man, whoever he was, had come hunting, come wanting to kill without warning from ambush. Morgan hoped he was still there. He wanted to pull the strings and see the sniper jerk.

Who? He wondered as he worked his way upslope, his boots silent against the hard earth. Sheriff Flowers and his men? It seemed unlikely that the sheriff would try to ambush him, but it was possible. Apaches? It was not their way to fire once and hide.

The answer seemed more complicated—or perhaps more simple. There was only one man he knew of who wanted him dead, who would have no qualms about killing from ambush. Able Sharpe.

How Sharpe could have found him up here was another problem. Shelter had no more time to ponder it. He was nearly on top of the sniper.

He saw the dark, bulky shape of a horse, head bowed, nibbling at the underbrush. The animal's head came up and it looked curiously at Shell but did not whicker, alarming its master.

Shell crept through the trees, staying in a low crouch, moving from tree to tree only after searching the ground ahead of him minutely.

There was a sudden flash of silver, sudden motion and the man loomed up out of the brush directly in Shelter's path. The rifle in his hands barked, stabbing crimson flame at Morgan.

But Shell was already moving, rolling away, snapping two loads from his .44 in the direction of the rifleman. One of those bullets tagged home. There was a savage ricochet as the hot lead struck metal, clanging loudly, then a cry of tortured pain.

Still Shelter held his position, listening to the empty night, the groaning of a man who might or might not have been playing possum.

Finally there were no more sounds and Morgan, circling wide toward the clump of brush came upon him.

He wasn't playing possum.

He was dead from a .44 slug through the heart. The sniper's mouth hung open in a kind of shocked awe. They never understood, it seemed, that they could die as well as their victims. His hands were still wrapped around a new .30 caliber Winchester repeater. His face was chalk white in the starlight. There was a smear of dark purple beside his mouth where he had coughed up blood.

It was not Able Sharpe, but Morgan had no idea who it was.

At the sound of approaching footsteps he whirled, palmed his Colt and went to a knee. The shadowy figure rushed out of the darkness toward him and Shelter, cursing, rose.

"I told you to stay back there," he growled. But Coral was into his arms already and it was difficult to stay angry.

"I had to know what happened," she said into Shelter's chest.

"All right." Shelter stepped back. "Will you look at him? See if you recognize him. And keep your voice down still—he probably was alone, but you can't be sure."

Coral nodded and then stepoed forward to look at

the dead man sprawled against the dark earth at Shelter's feet.

"I don't know him."

"Well, that's that then." Morgan searched the body, expecting to find nothing, finding nothing. It was the same with the man's saddlebags. The buckskin horse he had been riding wore a stable brand, but it was not from Rembrandt, and was likely stolen.

"I'm collecting horses right and left," Shell cracked. "Before you know it, I'll be ranching like your Mister Brunner."

They returned silently to the underground home of Coral Scant. Shell took a quick turn around the area, seeing nothing but a hunting owl.

"I'm not sure I like being down there," he told Coral. "If anyone ever comes up on you, finds this place, you're dead. They'd just cave it in or start firing bullets until a ricochet found you. And it's a long ways from the mine."

"You want us to move out?"

"If you're planning on staying after tonight. If you still want to work that shaft."

"But you said it was crazy, mad. You said the ore couldn't be shipped out profitably."

"Do you want to do it, Coral?"

"I'm going to do it, Mister Morgan."

Her voice was determined even if it did crack when she said that. Shelter told her, "Then I'm going to help you."

"And Able Sharpe?"

"He's waited a lot of years, I guess he can wait a few months more."

Besides he hadn't the slightest notion where to look

now for Sharpe. And he was wounded. The sheriff was out there somewhere waiting for him if he came out of these hills.

There was something else. "I kind of like hanging around you, Coral. Something I can't put my finger on."

"Oh yes you can," she insisted stepping near enough to him so that Shelter did just that. "Any objection to spending one more night down in the house."

"I'd take it hard if I wasn't invited," he said, and Coral led off, getting down that rickety ladder quicker than a monkey.

Sunrise was a deep pink flush on low hanging clouds. The highlands were deep green and golden brown. Coral had her possessions packed—tools, clothing, food, a small iron stove which the mule balked at carrying. "She's spoiled," Coral said.

She too was glowing rosy pink this morning. It was a wonder. She hadn't had a whole lot of rest.

"What's first?" she asked Shelter as they trailed out, riding the two horses, leading the jenny mule.

"I can't do much digging yet. What we should do is find us some help. Any ideas?"

"I hate to bring strangers in."

"They'll find out sooner or later anyway. If you've got men you stand a better chance of fighting off any claim jumpers. If you don't have some help, it won't matter. You'll be bringing up a teaspoon of ore a day without some men and picks."

"There's Agua Caliente," Coral said thoughtfully.

"What's that?"

"A Mexican town. It's in the States, I mean, but all

84

the people there are Mexican. They were there before there was a boundary and it doesn't mean a thing to them one way or the other."

"You know people there?"

"Some. Father and I used to trade there. One year when he went north he left me in the little church school at Caliente. But we don't have anything to pay men with."

"That'll work out. We can sell the buckskin. And," he nodded, "that iron stove."

"I cook on that!"

"We'll just have to teach you some new techniques. It's too bulky to tote around and not necessary. How far to Caliente?"

"Thirty miles or so. Southwest across the desert. Do you mean to go today?"

"I do. We need men to get started and I mean to get started as soon as possible."

The ride was hot, dry, but untroubled. They saw no sign of anyone, white or Apache until shortly before dusk they spotted the low adobe town of Agua Caliente named for the hot springs which burbled up in the town plaza.

Within an hour Shelter had sold the buckskin and its saddle for forty dollars. The iron stove brought an amused smile to the lips of one of the town traders. "But" he said, "my wife she thinks only rich people have such a thing. For her sake," he shrugged, "ten dollars American."

Coral started to object to the price, but Shell closed the deal. "We've toted that thing far enough."

They spent the night in separate rooms in the back of a little cantina where a guitarist played softly through the night and a woman in a black dress with slashing eyes danced on a saucer-sized stage.

Breakfast was eggs with bits of tortilla and spicy green chili pepers mixed in. Then they went out into the morning heat. Children played around the plaza where the hot springs burbled lazily. Red, unglazed tile formed a circular walkway and three newly painted green benches sat at intervals facing the spring.

The mustached, scarred man who lazed on the first of these benches rose as Coral and Shell approached. He was big, bowlegged, thick through the chest. He wore a white peon's costume, faded and torn, a red scarf around his dark throat and a floppy off-white sombrero. A long bladed knife rode on his hip, the handle shaped like an eagle head.

Shelter let his hand drift near to the butt of his holstered Colt as the big Mexican sauntered toward them, his obsidian eyes fixed on Coral.

"Co-ral!" he bellowed, arms outstretched and Coral halted, blinked and then smiled.

"Alejandro?"

"See," Alejandro said to the skies, "she does not even remember me. Yet I remember her, the lovely gringa who came to our pueblo to our school. I was so in love with her."

"It is you! My God, you were so skinny then."

"And now so fat," Alejandro said, although it was muscle and not fat which clung to his heavy bones. He removed his sombrero and stood looking at Coral deeply before he shot Shell a single, measuring glance. "I was ten when I saw you last, Co-ral, but I have not forgotten you, you see."

"I haven't forgotten you either, Alex, but you've changed so much."

"Ah, we all change," he said flashing a white smile. "This is your husband, I think?" His gaze was direct as he again turned it on Morgan.

"No. He is my friend and business partner."

"You are in business, Co-ral?"

"Well, in a way," she answered with a shrug of one shoulder. Then they sat down and she explained things to Alejandro Orta. He listened solemnly, nodding from time to time.

"That is dangerous country, Co-ral. Very bad. Muy Indios. Chiricahua. Very bad."

"Yes, it's true. But still we hoped to find two men who would work for us. We can pay a dollar a day for at least a month. I'd hoped that by then the laborers would see that we do have a rich claim, that I could persuade them to wait for their wages."

"I think Paco will go," Alejandro said. He stroked his chin thoughtfully. "Yes. He worked at the cantina but he was thrown out for being too drunk all the time."

"We can't use a drunk," Shell said.

"Paco drinks no more. It was only the temptation, you see," Alejandro said, flashing his even white teeth again in a smile that was somehow vaguely menacing. "He is strong for his size. Very willing."

"We can't refuse a man who is willing," Coral said. She looked at Shell who nodded. No, they couldn't refuse anyone who would work for them under their terms, in that country.

"All right. I'd like to talk to Paco. If we hire him on, we'll need just one more man."

87

"One more!" Alejandro laughed loudly. "You think I am going to leave Senorita Co-ral? No, it is deep love, and Alejandro must go along as well. Besides," he said in a more subdued tone, "I am without money. I have no job. There was a man who argued with Alejandro and called him a bad name." Now he was looking at Shelter again. "After I hurt him they did not want me on that job any more."

When Alejandro had gone to find Paco Coral said, "That business about him hurting someone—that didn't sound too good, did it? If you want, we can just forget Alejandro."

"No," Shell answered. "The man can fight, doesn't mind a scrap. It may come to a fight, I'd say we can use him. All that worried me," he said with a grin, putting his arm around Coral, "was that bit about it being deep love with Senorita Co-ral."

"He smelled like onions and garlic," Coral said. Her eyes glowed as she looked into Shell's ice-blue eyes. The sun beat down on the little plaza. "I've got the best, Shelter Morgan. Who needs the rest?"

8.

They rode north once more. Shelter Morgan on the sorrel, Coral Scant on her jenny mule looking tired and apprehensive now. Behind her rode the broad-shouldered Alejandro Orta and trailing, the silent, narrow Paco with his receding upper lip which revealed crooked, yellow teeth. He was morose and small, the hooked, swollen nose which over-hung a brush mustache, the only startling feature on an otherwise forgettable face.

He brightened only when Alejandro spoke to him as the big man's manner brightened only when Coral turned her eyes on Alejandro.

Shelter wasn't thrilled with them, but there was little choice. They simply didn't know Paco and Alejandro. Coral's schoolgirl acquaintance was meaningless as far as a character reference went. Morgan inconspicuously kept an eye on them, not wanting to discover too late that the Mexicans had taken this job in order to follow them out onto the empty desert, cut their throats and return with horses and cantina money.

"What is the matter, Business Partner," Alejandro asked finally, "you seem so worried to me."

"Just worried about the claim."

"Not about Alejandro?" the Mexican asked.

Shelter turned his cold blue eyes on Alejandro, giving him the message. "No, not about you. I don't think I have to worry about you, do I Alejandro?"

"No." The grin was gone. "No, señor, you do not have to worry about Alejandro."

Paco didn't say a word the entire ride. The little man looked as if he had been abducted or kicked hard in the groin. He definitely was not enthusiastic about this project. Alejandro seemed to have the man under complete control. The little one glowed whenever Alejandro spoke a word to him.

They came up on the claim site at sundown. Shelter hadn't seen the desert approach to the canyon before, and now that he was seeing it, he thought less of it than ever.

The sand was hock deep on the horses, concealing rocks. It was treacherous for wagons on the flats, impossible in the canyon itself.

Entering the mouth of the canyon as the skies darkened Morgan glanced up the steeply inclining walls of the rock-strewn landform, trying to imagine wagons hauling ore out of there. It took a lot of imagination.

They camped on a low outcropping, the fire burning low as Coral boiled coffee and fried bacon in a black iron pan. "We'll have to keep watch around the clock," Shell said. "Alejandro, after you eat, why don't you take the first shift. We'll pull it in four-hour stretches."

"All right, Business Partner," Alejandro said, his old sarcasm coming back.

90

Shelter ignored it. After eating bacon and sourdough bread Shell sat drinking coffee while Coral removed his shirt and examined his chest wound.

The compress was soaked with blood, but the wound itself seemed to be healing well enough. Alejandro, squatting with his own cup of coffee near the low fire peered at Shell and asked:

"What happened to you, Business Partner?"

"Squirrel bite," Shell replied.

"Ah." But Alejandro, his eyes searching Shell's hard torso, seeing the old scars, realized that he was in the presence of a fighting man. He reappraised Shelter Morgan, noticing the hands, broad and powerful, the hard set of his jaw, the icy eyes. His weapons were well-cared for, always close at hand. Alejandro, noticing all of this turned away and looked at Paco, shaking his head almost imperceptibly.

At dawn they were at the mouth of the shaft, Alejandro standing looking at the thousands of tons of stone which covered the mine and the surrounding slope both above and below.

"Bad, very bad," he said. "Like someone never wanted it open again."

Coral glanced at Shell, but he was looking only at Alejandro.

"We will have to use much dynamite," the Mexican said.

"No dynamite," Shelter told him. "It would bring everyone for fifty miles down on us."

"It is no good without dynamite!" Alejandro said angrily.

"It is no good to die, my friend, and if the Apaches come we shall die."

"I think maybe there is someone else who might come Mister Shelter Morgan." Alejandro's black eyes narrowed. He smiled and it wasn't a pretty thing to see.

"Maybe you're right," Shell answered.

"It is worth it to you, Senorita Co-ral? There is something you believe worth all of this labor?"

"I'll show you the ore we have," she offered and the four of them went into the roofed-over hollow.

"Pretty! *Madre de Dios*," Alejandro said as he turned the chunk of ore he held over. "Ver' rich. Ver' high grade."

"That's what we're working for, Alex," Coral said eagerly. "You know we can only pay you for the first month, but after that you'll see just how rich the claim is, and I hope you'll stay on until we can deliver our first ore shipment."

"Oh, yes," Alejandro said, rising, smiling. "We will stay on, Co-ral. No, Paco?"

"Whatever you say," Paco said miserably. It was plain he would rather be at his old job in the Agua Caliente cantina, sneaking tequila when the boss wasn't looking.

"If you'll take the first watch, Shelter," Coral said, suddenly animated and confident, "we'll get to work. Alex and I will climb up on top of the slide and see exactly what needs to be done. All right, Alex?"

"Anything, Co-ral," he answered, turning suddenly oily.

"Paco, if you'll start clearing away the drift—stay out from under the big rocks. We'll be scrambling around up above."

Paco nodded somberly. He would be staying out from under. Definitely. He eyed the overhead boulders and gave a little involuntary shudder.

Morgan shouldered his rifle and walked out. He climbed a small knoll opposite the shaft entrance, almost treading on a dozing rattler, found himself a nook partly in the shade and began a slow, methodical search of the hill opposite, of the canyon and desert floor beyond.

Nothing. But then you didn't generally see an Apache until he was on top of you, and they were still out there. Waiting.

Shell saw Coral and Alejandro scrambling up onto the slide, saw Paco moving a handful of stone at a time. Nothing else stirred but a black buzzard far away over the flats, rising on heated wind currents to glide effortlessly across the gleaming desert.

By noon Coral had made her decision.

"We're going to start a second slide. It'll clear half of the big rocks away—or," she said with a small shake of her head, "it will close up the shaft permanently."

Shelter's eyes lifted to the huge pile of rubble, to the great yellow boulders which lay concealing the shaft, and he nodded.

"What do you want me to do, Coral?"

"Are you up to it?" she asked, nodding at his shoulder.

"If you need me."

"I'd like for us all to work on that rock there." Her pointing finger indicated a slab of stone shaped like an elongated thumb nearly thirty feet high which stood like a headstone among the smaller boulders halfway up the slope. "If I'm reading it right that rock's keyed into the larger mass upslope. If we can topple it, we'll break loose most of the weight up there."

"And it all comes rushing down."

"I wouldn't want to be below it," Coral agreed.

"We'll have to use the horses and lines?"

"Yes. You wouldn't want to be out on the slope when it goes. If it goes."

Like most projects it was easier said than done. To get the horses up behind the uptilted slab they had to detour around three miles and come down the gentler slope above the landslide. It took another two hours to work their way out across the jumbled graveyard to the massive rock Coral had pegged as the keystone.

Shelter lassoed the stone like a great bull's neck and tightened down. They used three lines strung back upslope to where two horses and the jenny mule stood uneasily on the steep incline.

"This cannot work," Paco grumbled. He was slick with sweat from scrambling over the sun heated rocks.

"It better," Shell said.

"If it doesn't you're out of a job, Paco," Coral said lightly. The small man just stared at her with morose eyes. No matter what Alejandro had said, the little man was suffering—he needed a drink and badly.

The lines were drawn taut. Shell, up on the sorrel, hitched his rope around the pommel and backed the horse until the heavy line lifted from the rocks and the sorrel stood braced, legs trembling.

Coral backed her jenny expertly and her line too rose from the stones. Alejandro had trouble with his horse which wanted no part of this. He beat its head brutally with his fist, narrowing Shell's eyes with distaste, but eventually got his rope up. Paco took off upslope to stand fifty yards away just watching.

"All right," Coral said quietly and together they pulled.

94

The sorrel slipped, lurched forward and then backed again under Shelter's urging hand. Nothing was giving. He saw Coral's face rigid with emotion, the skin stretched taut over her fine cheekbones, her lower lip drawn in as she urged the jenny to strain against the immovable object.

The sorrel beneath Shell blew, tossed its head and tried again, its footing uneven on the steep slope, its eyes wide with effort and confusion.

Shell looked down at the ground, saw his horse's left forehoof make a new impression six inches farther upslope than before. He kneed it and again a new impression. The sorrel was gradually pawing its way upslope. Something was giving!

He swivelled his head, trying to see if the rope was creeping up the rock, but no, it was looped securely.

"It's moving," Shelter said.

"Nothing is happening!" Alejandro said angrily.

"It's moving, damnit," Shell shot back. "Keep it taut."

And then there was no doubt about it. Shell's sorrel lurched ahead a full foot and Morgan looking across his shoulder saw the big rock begin to slant toward him, saw it begin its slow inexorable motion earthward as gravity clawed at it.

"Here it comes," Shelter said and then he just sat the winded sorrel, watching. The huge monolith hit the ground, raising a storm of dust. But nothing else gave.

For the moment. There was a split second when Coral's face fell with disappointment, with weariness. And then her hand came up, her mouth opened in a thrilled shout.

"It's all going!" she cried.

And she was right. Gradually the displaced rocks before and beside the keystone began to slide off down the declivity before them. Then they gained impetus and the ground beneath Shell rumbled as the gigantic rockslide sloughed off, thundering down past the closed mine shaft, boulders bounding high into the air, clattering together, a column of yellow dust rising like smoke into the clear desert air.

When it had settled they made their way around, back to the shaft site. The shaft itself was buried once more under tons of rock, but the slope above was neatly cleared except for a handful of scattered boulders.

Coral leaped from her mule, stood hands at her sides for a moment and then jumped into the air, a happy yell escaping her lips. Alejandro, grinning beneath his drooping black mustache was beside her and he threw his arms around her, lifting her into the air, spinning her around.

"Success!" the Mexican shouted. He put Coral down and held her a little too long until Coral's expression turned uncomfortable and she shook free.

"Let's have a closer look," she said not looking at Alejandro who stood watching her still, glancing once, challengingly at Shelter Morgan.

There was definitely a feeling beyond that for an old school chum worming its slow way into Alejandro's mind. That was all they needed, Shelter thought sourly. He walked toward the vanished shaft, ignoring Alejandro.

"Well?" he asked as he reached Coral who stood in the settling dust, hands on hips, head thrown back to study the slope above.

"We won the gamble, Shell. There's a lot of rock

l.re to clear away, but we don't have that overhang now. No worry about everything caving in."

Not in that sense, perhaps. Yet the feeling persisted. Morgan felt that sooner or later everything was going to cave in, and when it did, it was going to come with a hell of a lot more thunder and destruction than a rockslide.

It was difficult to define—this uneasy feeling, but he saw it reflected everywhere. On the barren, Apache infested slopes, on the trackless desert, in the dark brooding eyes of Alejandro Orta.

He said nothing about it now. He watched as Coral glowed, feeling finally that her goal was within reach.

"Well," she said, "we've got a lot of daylight left. How about it, men!"

They got to it then, moving stone from over the shaft mouth. Or Alejandro and Paco did. Shell with his chest wound was good for nothing yet but sitting watch.

Truthfully his chest was feeling much better. He was healing well and quickly. He thought it best not to let Alejandro know that yet. He preferred sitting watch, rifle in hand, the two laborers below him and in sight. It beat the hell out of having them sitting above him with a gun.

Slowly the shaft was cleared. By the second day they had again uncovered timbering. The header had given in the recent slide, but without the mass of rock on top of it it could now be easily replaced. There was still some gray, weathered timber left near the mine, hidden back among the rocks by Coral's father and this could be used for the header and any necessary interior repairs.

"What's the matter with him?" Shell asked at noon

when he came in for a cup of coffee and some pan-made sourdough.

Paco was sagged in the thin shade cast by a low boulder, his face glistening with sweat, his eyes dark and unhappy.

"Just tired, I guess. We all are," Coral answered, handing Shell his cup.

"I'm getting a little tired of having all this company around," Shell told her and she smiled, touching his sleeve.

"Maybe we can do something about that. Tonight?"

"Tonight. Up on the ledge." Shelter said, nodding toward the high outcropping where they had first made love. Coral's eyes brightened, her breath seemed shallow and quick.

"When?"

"Midnight? After Paco goes on watch duty."

"Yes," she whispered breathily. Her fingers tightened on Shell's arm and he bent his head to kiss her forehead.

"All right," he said, "business now. Alejandro will get himself stirred up."

"He doesn't think of me in that way."

"The hell he doesn't—and if he didn't he'd be a fool." Together they walked to where the shaft mouth was now visible, the earth around it scoured with the signs of work. The timber for the new header lay to one side.

Shell bent his head and looked inside. They had gone in fifteen feet already, as far as they dared without replacing the shattered timber.

"Any color showing yet?"

"No," Coral answered. "Another fifteen feet or so,

think, before we will see the vein. It won't be that long, actually. You can see there's only loose rubble and that one big stone in our way. Then all we have to do is replace the header and we can start working the ore."

"Have you thought about getting wagons and a team yet?"

"Yes, as a matter of fact," Coral said as they walked away from the shaft. "I'm going to see Carl Brunner."

"Ah, the old boyfriend," Shelter teased.

"Stop that," she laughed.

"Once you've done that, whether you manage to get the wagons or not, everyone will know you're working the lost mine."

"Carl wouldn't tell a soul if I asked him not to."

"You trust him that much?"

"Yes. Yes, I do. If it hadn't been for Carl Brunner carrying us through one winter when Father was completely broke, we never would have found this mine at all. I rather think we might have starved to death," she said, laughing without much humor. "Father and I shared a stubbornness. He thought he had found something and he wouldn't leave the claim, starvation or not."

"Tell me about his death."

They had come to a small hollow overlooking the canyon. There the scent of cedars drifted down on the dry breeze from the highlands. Coral looked at Shell.

"I've told you already."

"Not in much detail."

"Well, there isn't much to tell, really." She leaned against a streaked boulder, hands behind her, her dark eyes thoughtful, looking out across the canyon. "Father had come up to the claim while I cleaned up after breakfast. I was a good hour or so coming up here and when I reached the mine he wasn't here which was odd, if you knew Father. When he said he was going to work, he went to work. I never could get him to slow down, you know. He was convinced he only had so much time, that this was his big chance . . . but he wasn't at the mine. Nor was his horse, a big blue roan which was blind in one eye."

"You looked for him."

"Of course. Not at first. I thought maybe he'd gone to the basin there." She pointed. "After a rain it catches water and he used to leave his horse there. But after another hour I started looking."

Coral's voice broke. She bit at her lip and went on determinedly. "I didn't really know where to start. After all, there is no place near around that he would have gone to for any reason."

That was true. What purpose had Scant had for leaving the claim? "Where did you find him?"

"Over the ridge. Near the Rembrandt trail. God knows why he was over there. He couldn't have been on his way to town. For what purpose? He had come to work that morning. I might never have found him except I heard the roan and saw it coming back down the trail to the basin, reins dragging. I backtracked it and found . . . Father."

"He was dead already?"

"Dead. Yes. He had been scalped, but it wasn't an Apache who did it. I know that, Shelter! It was a crude trick."

"How do you know—sorry, Coral, but I'm trying to understand this."

"Because," she gulped dryly, "I found the scalp

100

buried alongside the trail on the way to Rembrandt. Do you think an Apache scalps an enemy and then buries the scalp Shell? No. It was a white man."

"But why?"

"Because of the mine."

"Maybe, but it doesn't make much sense to have killed him before they had discovered where the mine was."

"I'll tell you what I believe, Shell. Maybe I'm wrong, but I think they came up here looking for the mine. Father was someone riding the Rembrandt trail and went out to meet them. Maybe there was an argument. Father would have refused to tell them anything, of course. Maybe they meant to torture him, maybe the knife slipped. But they killed him before he told them where the mine was."

"Or," Shell suggested, "he did tell them and was killed. But after his death you caved the mine in, and they knew they couldn't clear it off without attracting a deal of attention—buying dynamite for instance would tip a lot of people to what was happening, to who had killed your father."

"Maybe. I don't know. What does it matter now, Shelter? What does it matter!"

"It matters because your father was killed over this claim, because you've opened it again now. He was killed and whoever killed him is still around, waiting to kill again if necessary."

And that was prophecy. The uneasy feeling Shelter had tried to fight off was going to take on hard substance too soon.

9.

The night was cold on the ledge. Stars glittered in a velvet sky and the rim of a coming moon cast a pale glow on the flats. The canyon below Shell was deep in velvety shadow. A nighthawk cried distantly. Coral shifted and he smiled in the darkness.

Her hands dipped between his legs, hefting him, measuring him with pleasure as her own legs spread still wider and she drew him in again, her eyes alive with starlight.

Shell's hand roamed across her firm breasts and his lips met hers as she sighed, her feet locking together behind his ass, nudging him in a steady, lazy rhythm.

Minutes ago she had finished with a rousing, wrenching climax, her eyes wide, mouth sagged open, hands tearing at Shell, her hips writhing, her body twisting and shuddering.

Now she was at ease, a slow liquid warmth seeping from her, but still she wanted to feel him, to have him sliding in and out of her, to touch his heavy sack as it nudged against her, to feel his lips working against her taut nipples.

The horrified scream echoing up the deep canyon brought them both sharply alert, their tender feelings cut off as if by a knife.

Shell dove for his Colt and came to his feet in the darkness, Coral clinging to his naked leg, her face against his hard buttock.

"What . . . ?" she whispered, her breath warm against his thigh, her fingers clutching at him.

"Ssh!" He touched her head with his hand. There was a sound still below them, far below. The pitiful sobbing of a man in fear. Then the strangled shriek again, a gurgling whimper.

Then silence.

"My God," Coral Scant said before Shelter could silence her.

"Stay here," he said, bending over. "Be quiet."

"You're not going to leave me?" Her voice held panic.

"Get dressed. Get on that jenny mule and be ready to ride."

"Apaches?"

"I don't know," Shell hissed, pulling on his pants, stamping into his boots. He paused to kiss Coral, to remind her, "Get dressed and be ready to ride."

Then he pulled away from her and began working his way down the canyon, not mounted but afoot. The sorrel crashing through that brush would make enough noise to wake the dead. And add one more to their numbers.

He plunged downslope, Colt in hand, trying to move both quickly and cautiously. The canyon was plunged in darkness, the brush caught at his legs; a branch struck him across the forehead.

He paid no attention. His thoughts were on life and death. On the enemy who lurked in the darkness somewhere. Approaching the claim Shell slowed his pace deliberately, creeping forward with shadowy stealth.

The campfire still showed as dully glowing embers which cast faint illumination on the shaft entrance—and on the mutilated body which lay in the center of the clearing.

It was Paco, lying in a black pool which was his blood. His throat had been opened from ear to ear, his eyes gouged out. His scalp had been taken.

Something moved in the underbrush across the clearing and Shell went lower, pressing himself against the earth, his hand cramped and perspiring as it gripped the Colt, his thumb locked over the curved hammer.

Nothing moved. He didn't dare flinch, take a deep breath. His muscles knotted and his vision grew blurry. Still he did not move as the minutes crept painfully past.

Then the sound across the clearing took on shadowy substance, loomed up and crept forward. It was Alejandro, rifle in his hands and he moved in a crouch to where Paco lay. His face was lost in shadows and Shell could not see the expression on the Mexican's face.

"Hold it, Alejandro," he said in a low voice which carried well in the night.

"Morgan?"

"That's right. Put down the rifle."

Alejandro did so, with extreme caution. He stayed in his deep crouch, moving not a muscle. Shell came

104

up then, eyes flickering from side to side, back to Alejandro who had not twitched.

"All right," Shell said, "get up."

"You going to kill me too?" Alejandro asked, his voice a low growl.

"Kill you?"

"What's the matter, Morgan? Now you got the shaft cleared, you don't need us no more? Now you going to have all this gold for yourself."

"Shut up, Alejandro."

The Mexican had continued walking forward. Now he stood a yard from the muzzle of Shell's pistol, hands at shoulder height, eyes lost in deep shadows. The moon was rising behind Alejandro, a diffused golden glow staining the horizon.

"I didn't kill him," Morgan said.

"No? Who then, amigo?"

"Maybe you, Alejandro. Maybe you. You were down here."

"Me!" Alejandro seemed genuinely outraged, but then Shelter had already decided the man was a good actor.

"Maybe Chiricahuas."

Alejandro seemed to flinch at that suggestion. He looked around him. "Give me my gun back."

"No."

"If they're out there . . ."

"I don't think they are. Do you, Alejandro?"

"What's happened?" Coral rushed into the clearing stopped and gasped, turning away from the mutilated body of Paco which was still against the ground, grinning up at them.

"Don't you ever stay where I put you," Shelter said

with some irritation.

"Who did it?" she asked weakly.

"Alejandro thinks it was me," Shell answered. His eyes hadn't left the Mexican. His thumb was still on the hammer of his big single-action .44.

"Didn't you tell him?" Coral asked.

"No. He didn't ask."

"Tell me what?" Alejandro demanded.

"Shelter was with me when we heard the scream. He couldn't have done it, Alejandro. Besides, he's not that sort of man."

But was Alejandro Orta that kind of man? It didn't figure, really. Paco was his friend, at least on the surface. What was to be gained by killing the inoffensive little man?

Alejandro's thoughts were working down the same channels. "I have no reason to do such a thing, Coral." He spread his hands and shrugged massively. "It was not me. But there is someone around who does this. Give me back my gun. I think I will need it soon."

"Shell?"

"All right," Morgan agreed after a minute. He puffed out a stream of breath and lowered his gun. "Go ahead."

"You are kind, Morgan," Alejandro said with deep sarcasm. He stooped over and picked up his gun, glowering at Shelter still, still apparently wondering. Wondering who had done it.

"If it had been Apaches, they'd be all over us by now," Shell commented.

"It could have been one man," Coral offered.

"Maybe."

106

Shell crossed to where Paco lay, thumbed a match to life and examined the body by its wavering red glare. Coral gasped again and Shelter glanced at her sharply.

"What is it?"

"Nothing. Maybe nothing, but—Shelter, that's exactly the way I found my Father!"

When they began work the next morning, it was with guns near at hand and their eyes constantly searching the surrounding hills for trouble. There was trouble out there, you could smell it, sense it hovering overhead. It was a dirty, hollow feeling in the pit of Shell's gut.

He had no trust for Alejandro who worked side by side with him moving rock from the shaft. Alejandro who was silent and scowling, his dark eyes not leaving Shelter except when absolutely necessary.

Work proceeded slowly. Coral spent the daylight hours at lookout atop the claim. Alejandro and Shell slowly worked their way into the shaft. Morgan's chest was healed enough to allow him to use pick and shovel now although his strength was down.

After three days of hauling rubble on a low, crudely built sledge the shaft was clear enough to allow the re-timbering of the main tunnel.

"Look at it," Coral said as she inspected by lantern-light.

Morgan shook his head. It was rich, all right. Rich beyond his expectations if not beyond Coral's. A network of fine veins spider-webbed the quartzite cavern. Where they came together near the floor of the present shaft a widening wedge of color indicated a seam of high grade angling downward. They could see where

107

Aaron Scant had begun to dig a following shaft before death had snuffed out his plans.

The gold shone in the lanternlight, gleaming yellow. Only Alejandro's eyes gleamed brighter. He couldn't hide the avarice in those eyes. Dollar-a-day wages weren't going to satisfy this man.

"There will be a share for you too," Coral told him after they had emerged from the shaft into the brittle, harsh daylight.

"Whatever you wish, Co-ral," the Mexican said unconvincingly.

"I wish you to have a share, Alejandro. And there will be something for Paco's family if he had one."

"First we'd better figure out how we're going to turn any kind of profit," Shell said. "We need a wagon at the least. Truth is we need a dozen wagons, a dozen men and a couple dozen horses."

"We need a wagon," Coral said. "Think big, but start small."

"Any ideas?"

"Yes. Carl Brunner."

"Kind of thought that might be it." Shell nodded. "All right. Alejandro, let's get us a ton of the best ore we can pick out of there."

And they did. It was gruelling work, a week of it, the temperature in the close environment of the mine shaft crippling at mid-day as the desert sun glared down. Picks broke, dulled, there were two small cave-ins, one of which pinned Alejandro briefly, but he escaped with only a badly bruised leg. The ore was dragged to the shaft entrance and dumped down the incline to the ledge where it was possible they would be able to build a ramp for an ore wagon.

At dusk the two men hardly had the strength to speak. They sat gloomily near the campfire, staring at each other mistrustfully. Then the luckier of the two would take his turn to sleep while the other stood night watch. Four hours of that after a day's digging and a man fell into a soundless, unmoving, nearly unconscious sleep.

Yet at the end of the week they had a load of ore, and very high-grade stuff indeed. Some of it could have been cleaned by hand, picking the gold from the surrounding quartz with a penknife.

"It doesn't show any sign of petering out," Shell told Coral. "That vein keeps widening out." He sketched it in the sand. "It jogs up, following that hard seam of shale for a ways before the shale breaks up in that fracture. Then down it goes again, widening out an inch for every foot you follow it down."

"My father knew what he was doing."

"It seems so." Shell rose, dusting his hands. "This will set you up for life, Coral. Give you all you need to be comfortable and happy."

"All?" Her eyes sparkled as she stepped nearer, her hand resting on his waist. Shell hugged her briefly and smiled, but Coral read that smile correctly and it did nothing to lift her spirits. He would not be staying. Not Shelter Morgan. He had trails to travel, men to hunt. He was here for a time and then he would be gone. She knew it and she knew she had to accept it.

"We're ready," Shelter said. "Time to get us a wagon and team and haul out of here."

"And now," Coral said, "you expect the real trouble to begin, don't you?"

"Yes, I do. You've opened the door to the vault. All

109

they've got to do is step up and help themselves."

"Alejandro!" Coral called to the big Mexican whose face was covered with dirt, sweat and a new growth of beard. He got heavily to his feet and walked to where Shell and Coral stood.

"Si, Co-ral?"

"We're going to have to leave you alone up here."

"Oh?" His eyes shifted from Coral to Shell and back again.

"We're going to get a wagon and perhaps a team. I'm taking Shelter to drive it back. Watch yourself." She briefly took his scarred, thick hand, "Please?"

"All right." Alejandro brightened briefly. He took a deep breath, looking at the rising boulder-strewn hills around them. "I will be here when you return."

Shell stood leaning against a boulder, watching the Mexican. Maybe he would be here, and then maybe he would fill his saddlebags with the best of the ore and hightail it out of there. That wouldn't hurt Morgan's feelings a bit.

What Alejandro's thoughts were Shell could not read in those black eyes. His scarred face remained expressionless as Coral and Shelter began to saddle up and ride out toward the Carrizo and the horse ranch of Carl Brunner.

Alejandro had begun packing a small pack of his own. "I will not be down here, Co-ral," he told her. "In the rocks on the far side. You know the small cave?"

"Yes."

"Good." Alejandro nodded, watched as they mounted and walked their horses out down the canyon. Then he shouldered his pack and started up the canyon wall toward the tiny cave where he would hold out until their return.

Shell saw Alejandro begin his climb, then he returned his thoughts to the task at hand. He eyed the canyon floor as they rode out toward the desert, trying to find a route the wagon could use to reach the shaft.

"Well?" Coral interrupted his thoughts. "Will he stick?"

"We're not losing much if he doesn't."

"You don't like him, do you?"

"Not much."

That effectively ended the conversation. In another half hour they were out onto the desert itself, the sun lancing down on back and shoulders, hands and necks, glaring off the sand, drying throats and mouths.

Coral led the way to the Carrizo which was a dry reddish wash winding through stunted willows and broken, dusty cotton-woods. Away from the thin vaguely green band of brush along the river there was nothing growing. Nothing but the yucca and crimson-tipped, thorny ocotillo.

Shell tugged his hat lower, seeing nothing but empty land, a smoky mesa far distant, the ears of his sorrel.

Nothing until the Apaches rose out of the sand like painted demons out of the bowels of the earth and the guns opened up on them.

10.

The jenny mule went down with a loud protesting bray, its right foreleg shattered by an Apache bullet. The mule went over head first and Coral, clinging to the saddlehorn, went with it. The mule landed hard, pinning Coral beneath it as it struggled futilely to rise.

Morgan saw all of this from the corner of his eye and he cursed violently. He had his sorrel turned and set to run, had his Winchester up and shouldered. Now he had to set the brakes, wheel the horse around and face the fire of the onrushing Apaches.

A bullet whipped past Shell's ear as he fired off-handedly at the nearest Apache. The bullet caught the Indian's skull and the Chiricahua's face vanished in a red mist as the .44-40 bullet disintegrated bone and flesh.

Shell dismounted at the run and threw himself to his belly. The sorrel danced free and galloped across the desert, trailing its reins.

Shell spotted a darting Apache to his left and switched his sights, but before he could pull off the Indian had vanished again. They were ghosts, these men, desert fighters, skilled guerillas. They had held back the best the US Army had to offer for years under great leaders like Cochise and Geronimo. Warfare was a way of life with them, and they knew what they were doing here on their home ground.

Morgan admitted all of that, affirmed it, but vowed that no matter who they were, how good, he wasn't going to doubt his own abilities. Doubt led to defeat.

So did overconfidence.

A Chiricahua brave, weirdly painted with snaking yellow and white lines spotted Coral pinned beneath her mule and determined that she was easy pickings. By tonight he would have a white woman prisoner.

By tonight he would be in the Bright Land beyond this earth. Coral's rifle was in her hands and she fired from her awkward position as the Apache warrior made his dash toward her.

His head was thrown back exultantly. He yelled shrilly as he rushed forward. Coral's Winchester barked unexpectedly and the warrior met the spinning white-hot lead from her rifle's muzzle. It entered just below the breastbone and went right on through bone and gut to splinter the Indian's backbone, killing him instantly.

Shell saw that, simultaneously felt rather than saw a new threat behind him. He rolled onto his back and fired his rifle as the Apache leaped at him, knife drawn.

The Indian was already too close as the rifle exploded. The bullet whipped harmlessly past his shoulder and Shell had to roll away as the mirror-like blade of the Apache's knife cut past his skull so near that it sheared away a handful of hair.

Morgan drew his Colt without thinking about it. An automatic instinct, it saved his life. He jabbed the muzzle of the .44 into the Apache's ribs and triggered off, feeling the Indian's body leap as the slug penetrated, destroying innards and muscles.

The knife, poised for a second downstroke, fell feebly as the Indian died, and Shelter rolled the corpse aside, coming to one knee to trigger off again.

A small, flat-faced Apache had circled Coral's downed mule and was coming up on her, moving with incredible speed and stealth in a low crouch. Shell fired from his knee, holding the big blue Colt in a two-handed grip.

His first shot shattered hip and buttock and the Apache screamed with pain, half spinning as he went down, Shell's next shot catching him before he hit the ground, impacting into the Indian's skull which exploded like a ripe melon, spattering brain and bone.

The desert was suddenly still and Shell took the moment to thumb fresh loads into his weapons. Sweat rained off him. His eyes were red, raw as they swept the desert flats, seeking targets.

Nothing.

No one stirred. It was if there had never been another living thing on those red flats. Except for the sprawled corpses of the fallen warriors.

Shell shuttled across to where Coral lay trying frantically to free herself from the weight of the downed jenny mule. Morgan slit the mule's throat with his bowie, not wanting the panicked, injured animal to roll and crush Coral or cut Shell to ribbons with those razor-edged hoofs.

Coral winced as he did it as if she herself had been cut. She knew it was necessary and merciful, however and there was no reproach in her eyes.

"Where are they?" she whispered.

"I don't know. Quiet."

He dug out sand from beneath Coral's leg and pulled her free of the mule. It was damnably hot on the flats. Shell's head spun, dancing with colored lights.

"Where are they?" Coral asked again, coming shakily to her feet. "Why did they pull off?"

"I don't know," Shelter repeated, but in a moment he did know. "Look."

Coral followed his pointing finger. A cloud of dust was drifting toward them from the north. Horsemen, and many of them. "Soldiers?" she asked.

"I don't think so." Shell took her arm. "Come on."

With canteens and rifles in hand they headed into the tangle of brush in the Carrizo wash. Shelter went to his belly and pulled Coral after him. She was startled into protest, but Morgan got his hand over her mouth.

"What is it?" she said with eyes alone and Shelter shook his head, leading off on his belly into the deepest brush.

Panting, soaked in perspiration they crawled up onto a sand island—or what was an island when the Carrizo ran which was seldom this far south.

Parting the willow brush with his hand Shell peered through the brush and the gathering swarms of gnats to watch the approaching horsemen, Coral clinging to his arm, her breath coming in dry gasps, her blouse torn, a long scratch on her cheek bleeding.

Her lips grazed his ear. "Who are they?"

Shell said nothing and Coral returned her gaze to the flats where the horsemen neared through the distorting veil of rising heat waves.

115

Ten, fifteen, sixteen men and from that distance Coral could recognize none of them. But she could see now, as Shell had the small shimmering mirror on the shirtfront of the leading rider. He was wearing a badge and they were looking for someone.

Shelter Morgan.

"Holy Christ!" someone said loudly enough for the words to reach them in their thicket.

Hands reached for rifles and pulled them free of scabbards. "Easy now. We got Apaches."

"See anyone?"

"No, and I don't want to." That voice was Sheriff Colin Flowers'.

"There's a mule down here," another man said. Small bootprints. Awful like a woman's, Sheriff."

"Son of a bitch," Flowers grumbled. They could see him remove his hat and wipe his forehead. "Anything else?"

"Lot of Indian moccasin tracks. Apache boots, for sure. Possibly a man here, Sheriff. Maybe a white man's tracks. Sign's all screwed up, can't be sure."

"Man and his wife?"

"Maybe."

"Who?"

"Folks out of Agua Caliente maybe. Man and his wife," the tracker guessed. "Apaches hit 'em. Likely they've got 'em prisoner now. Pity the woman."

"And damn the man who was fool enough to bring her out here."

Shell held his breath. His eyes swept across the desert, searching for, not wanting to see, the sorrel which Flowers would identify instantly.

One of the deputies had dismounted and, dropping

his reins was approaching the brush-clotted wash, rifle in hands. Had he seen something? Shelter couldn't read the man's eyes, hidden as they were in the shadow of his hat brim. He was young, stocky and determined looking.

"Where the hell you going, Ed?" the sheriff asked. The kid stopped and glanced back at the lawman.

"In there, Sheriff Flowers."

"Just poke around a little?"

"That's right."

"You'll get your damned throat cut too if there's any Apaches left around here. They haven't been gone but a few minutes, Ed. Where in hell you think they got to?"

"They might have the woman in there," the kid said uncertainly. Shelter had to give the kid grudging admiration for his guts if not his brains. He hoped like hell the sheriff won this argument—he would hate to have to kill the deputy.

"If they got her, Ed, she's either dead or they got her under guard. I'm afraid you can't accomplish a thing, son."

The kid let his eyes sweep the wash once more. Shell saw his shoulders lift as he took a deep breath and nodded. "You're right, I guess. It just galls me, that's all."

"Losing your scalp will gall you even more," someone said and they laughed.

The posse mounted again and headed south. Shelter held Coral until they were out of sight, until even their dust had settled. He could feel her heart pounding beneath her ribs, and when he glanced at her she was still pale and shaken.

117

"Let's be on our way," he said, giving her a quick squeeze.

"They're looking for you," she said.

"That's right."

"I thought they would have given up by now."

"I don't think Flowers gives up easily."

"But they should have thought you were out of the country by now," she insisted as they rose cautiously.

"Yes," Shell agreed, "you'd think so."

"Unless someone saw you."

"Who? How could anyone have seen me?"

"There was one man who could have," she reminded him. "The man who killed Paco."

The man who killed Paco. The man who also killed Aaron Scant? A man who wanted that claim bad enough to come in as savage as any Chiricahua. A night hunter, a man skilled at his craft. Who?

They walked a mile north before they found the sorrel, head bowed, the reins all cut up by its hoofs as it trampled on them. It seemed glad to see them. It whickered softly.

Back in the saddle Shelter rode steadily northward, following the Carrizo where water now trickled, slowly seeping into the sands. The farther north they rode the more water ran through the narrow gorge until it became a fair-sized river and green grass spread out from its course.

Coral had clung silently to Shell, saying not a word. Now she straightened up.

"Another mile. Shell," she hesitated, "I don't think you ought to go in with me."

"Why not?"

"It's safer." The country was still alert for a man

matching Shelter Morgan's description.

"I have to agree with you. But tell me, can you manage that freight wagon."

"If I have to!"

"All right. Calm down. I want to go in with you, Coral. I have my reasons. Introduce me as a cousin from back East. Say I came out from Indiana with you. No one will question you. Likely Brunner will be so pleased to see you back he won't pay me any attention."

If he didn't already know that Coral was back.

If his name really was Carl Brunner.

That was the real reason Shelter wanted to go in. He had looked Rembrandt over thoroughly, not finding Able Sharpe. He hadn't gotten the opportunity to look around the outlying ranches after Sally was killed.

Benny Dierking had seen Able Sharpe riding into Rembrandt, he had said. Riding in from where? Maybe from the Rafter CB. At any rate, Shelter meant to have a look.

Coral had fallen silent again, seeing that her arguments were going to have no effect. Now he felt her shift, saw her pointing finger.

"There it is," she said with some excitement, and there it was indeed. Rafter CB. Set in a grassy valley where scattered live oaks and cottonwoods grew. A large horse herd grazed on the sparse green grass, and farther up the valley, Shell saw white-faced cattle. A white, two-story ranch house sat back behind a screen of oak trees. It was well kept up as were the outbuildings, the pole corrals. It was a business-like, well thought-out, well-maintained operation. *"Back home,"* Able Sharpe had said, *"Father keeps a hun-*

dred horses. All Arabian. Pride of Alabama, those horses are. Kept clean. You could eat off of our stable floor."

"Ready to go on down?" Coral asked.

"I'm ready," he answered grimly.

11.

They were intercepted by two ranch hands before they reached the yard. One of them was as old as the hills, with a silver mustache, sun-lined face, pale gray eyes. The other a quarter of his age with a shock of carrot-colored hair and the blank, belligerent expression of a dull maverick steer.

"Damn me!" the old man said. "Miss Scant."

"It's me, Jed."

"Lord have mercy!" The old man removed his hat. "Where in the world have you been?" His eyes narrowed, "And what's been happening to you! Lord, child, there's blood on your face."

"We tangled with a few Indians, Jed," she said. "Fortunately . . . Bob is a fair hand with a gun."

Jed's eyes switched to Shelter Morgan. The redheaded kid's eyes had never left him.

"Bob? Don't believe I know him."

"It's no wonder," Coral smiled. "Bob Winslow's my cousin from Indiana. That's where I've been, Jed. Staying with an aunt these past three years."

"Now, I did hear somethin' about that from Mister Brunner." He scratched his head. "Apaches, was they—damn the rascals. We'll have to look sharp, Harold."

Harold nodded, still looking blankly at Shelter.

"What was it you needed, Miss Scant?"

"Why, to see Mister Brunner."

"Gone, Miss. Into Rembrandt to talk horse swapping with some Eastern man—" Jed chuckled dryly, "and I do pity the man that ties up with Carl Brunner when it comes to horse trading."

"Maybe you could help me then, Jed," Coral went on. "What I wanted to do was to borrow the old freight wagon if you still have it. And a strong team."

"We still have the wagon. Don't use it but every fourth Saturday for hauling supplies out." Jed looked briefly puzzled, but said, "I wouldn't lend it out to nobody on my own say-so, Miss Scant, but Mister Brunner, he'd take it hard if I didn't let you have whatever you asked for. The wagon's yours. Maybe," he said, "you'd come into the house and write him a note so's he'd know it was you."

"Certainly, Jed." She glanced at Shelter. "Would you like to come along, Bob?"

"No. Maybe Harold can show me the wagon and harness. We can be all hitched by the time you're ready to go back home, Cousin Coral."

Shelter kept a perfectly straight face, but he was afraid Coral was going to break into a grin and give it away. Remembering the lynch rope which awaited Shell, she didn't.

"Let's go on then, Jed. Sorry to miss Mister Brunner."

"And he'll be terrible sorry to have missed you, Miss Scant. He'll be back this evening, I expect if you wanted to wait until supper time."

"No. I'd like to, but . . ."

Their voices faded away as they crossed the yard toward the big white house. Shell sat, hat tugged low, watching Harold who simply sat his horse, his dull expression set, cold.

"Want to show me that wagon?"

"Sure."

He looked like it was the last thing in the world he wanted to do, but he turned the paint pony he rode and Shelter followed along, looking over the ranch as they approached the massive green and white barn behind the oaks in back of the house.

"How many horses are you running?"

"Mister Brunner's got maybe six hundred head. Maybe a hundred of them are blooded." He glanced at the sorrel Shell was riding. "Where'd you come by that one?"

Shell's face remained expressionless. "He one of yours?"

"Was. Didn't you even look at that brand. Rafter CB."

"Is it? Belongs to my cousin. I don't know a thing about horses myself."

"Yeah, you sit it like you've never been on one," Harold said dryly. He might not have been the smartest man in the world, but there was a native shrewdness when it came to the things he knew—horses and horses.

"Didn't you sell this horse to Miss Scant?" Shell asked casually.

"*I* don't sell nothin'. As to who that sorrel was sold to, you'd have to ask Mister Brunner."

No luck there. Harold wasn't going to say who had been riding the sorrel before Shell had taken it the day the stage had been held up. Maybe he didn't know.

They had pulled up before the barn and Harold swung down easily, dropping the reins to his pinto. Shell followed him in to the cool vastness of the barn, smelling sweet hay and wood, leather and coal oil. Nothing was in disrepair, there was no dirt on the harness that hung from hooks on the wall. The high-wheeled wagon was newly painted. Green with yellow wheels decorated with black pinstripes.

The stable was so clean you could eat off the floor.

"This is it. See you return it in the shape it's in," Harold said and Shell nodded his head meekly.

"The boss likes things clean?"

"You bet. Neat and clean. That's Mister Brunner."

"You know, I think I met him once down in Socorro," Shell hazarded as Harold got the harness down from the wall.

"That so?"

"I'm not sure. It was a horse deal. Isn't he tall, dark haired. Kind of piercing eyes."

"Mister Brunner? Hell, he's only got one eye, Bob. One eye, kind of a scarred-up face and hair as white as snow."

Shell felt his heart sink. He had been so sure—had had that feeling in the pit of his stomach. The description could not possibly match Able Sharpe, however, and there was no deceit evident in Harold's eyes.

"Guess it couldn't have been him," Shell said. "Maybe there's someone else on the place, someone

124

that would have been doing Rafter CB business."

"That looks like that? No, if there was trading to do it would be Mister Brunner himself or Jed." Harold shouldered the harness and walked to the wagon, draping it over the massive front left wheel. "Now if you want to come along back and pick you out a team of draw horses."

"Sure," Morgan said, feeling let down. In the corral there were some fine looking, big shouldered horses. Two of them showed indications of Percheron blood. Big, heavily muscled horses with shoulders at Shell's head level.

"They'll do for a start," Morgan said. "We need something with muscle."

"Take care of 'em," Harold said in a tone which indicated that if he were in charge of Rafter CB, no damned drifting cousin to a drifting female would borrow those Percherons.

Shell gravely vowed to take good care of the draft horses. He would hitch them as wheel horses, and there was a big gray and a stocky, wild-eyed bay which would do for the lead team. He selected them and Harold grew even more surly. They were apparently personal favorites.

Nevertheless he helped Shell lead the horses into the barn and hitch them.

"Ran into some 'Paches down south, did you?" Harold asked.

"That's right."

"Handle them all right?"

"Got lucky."

"Yeah." Harold straightened up from the chains. "Been a lot of happenings around here lately. Stage

125

held up a while back. Woman murdered in Rembrandt."

"That right?"

"Yeah, must've happened since you arrived."

"I guess someone did mention it," Shelter said, not liking the drift of the conversation.

"Sheriff was through here looking for a man earlier. Described him to me. Didn't look much different from you according to him."

"That so?" Shell smiled. "A lot of men look like me."

"I guess." After another long, appraising look at Shelter Morgan, Harold seemed to lose interest in that topic. He went back to the horses, telling Shelter how he ought to feed them, water them, curry them, watch their shoes, remembering the Percherons weren't cow ponies. Shelter listened with a serious expression, nodding his head from time to time.

"Ready?"

Coral Scant stood in the barn doorway, Jed beside her. Shelter took the reins from Harold and answered.

"More than ready. Tie that sorrel on back and let's get while we've got light."

Jed did the honors, tying the sorrel on behind, helping Coral up onto the high box of the big freight wagon.

"Mister Brunner'll be sorry he missed you, Coral. You'll be coming back soon, I expect."

"I hope so, Jed."

"Can I tell Mister Brunner where he can find you if he wants to come callin'?"

"Well—" Coral hesitated, "just tell him I'll be back in a few days. And . . . tell him I'm looking forward

126

to seeing him again. Three years has been too long."

"Yes, Miss Scant. I'll tell him." Jed had a puzzled—or was it worried?—expression on his sun-dried face. He stepped back, scratching his head as he looked at Shelter Morgan one last time before Shell snapped the reins and the big team lurched forward, drawing the wagon out into the yard.

They had gone a mile before either of them said anything. "Alejandro," Coral said at last.

"Yeah, I know."

The Apaches had fled southward, and they would know that the Mexican was there alone. Flowers too had been riding that way and Shell had no illusions—if Alejandro had the chance to turn Morgan over to the law, he would take it.

The wagon rolled on across the desert flats, its specially designed, wide wheels making going easier than Shell had hoped. Brunner knew what he was doing, Shelter had to admit. He had had his freight wagon designed with the sand in mind, had purchased some horses big enough to haul it. He didn't seem to miss much. Maybe he hadn't missed out on getting Coral Scant either. She was silent and withdrawn most of the trip home, her thoughts too obviously on Brunner.

At the foot of the canyon Shell halted the team. The sun was bleeding against the western sky, outlining the far mesa, the Dragoon Mountains with crimson fire. Dove winged homeward across a flaming desert sky.

"Why did you stop?"

"I'm going to have a look on foot," Shelter told her. He handed Coral the reins to the team and slipped from the box, taking his rifle with him.

The canyon was cooling rapidly. It was dead silent, empty of all life. Well, not quite.

"Hold it right there," the familiar voice whispered.

"It's me, Alejandro. Morgan."

The Mexican came forward out of the shadows, his rifle leveled at Shell's belly. He grunted and lowered the weapon.

"Didn't expect you on foot. Where's Co-ral?"

"Down below with the wagon. Any trouble while we were gone?"

"Nothing much. Saw a party of white men. They looked up here, didn't search much. Heard some guns."

"That was us."

"Apaches?"

"That's right."

Alejandro sighed heavily. "Yeah, they're around. I smell them. Maybe I was wrong, Morgan. I thought the Apaches did not kill Paco."

"You weren't wrong," Shell said. "No, it wasn't me, but it wasn't the Indians either. You just watch yourself. There's someone around who doesn't want us up here."

"You worry about Alejandro!" he laughed.

"You're all we've got, my friend," Shell said soberly. "Come on. It'll take some work if we're going to get that wagon up the canyon before its full dark."

It took some work. Much detouring, some brush clearing, a temporary road made hastily with loose rock. The wagon almost rolled once, but by half an hour after dark they had the freight wagon to the shaft site, the horses grazing on the sparse brush, a low campfire burning.

"First watch?" Alejandro asked, finishing his coffee.

"I'll take it. You've got to be beat," Shell answered.

"Morgan—" Alejandro rose, shook his head and said, "Sometimes I don't think you are such a bastard after all." Then he turned and went to where he had his bedroll spread out.

Coral smiled. Softly she said, "Sometimes I don't think so either, Shelter Morgan."

Shell laughed and settled back on one elbow, watching Coral. She was weary but sparkling with eagerness. She was working toward her goal and despite the difficulties, it seemed she would make it.

"Why did they kill her?" Coral asked out of the blue.

"What?"

"The woman in Rembrandt—" she looked into the dying embers, her face shadowed, "why did they kill her, Shelter. If they wanted you dead, why go about it the way they did? Why kill her?"

"I think," Shell told her, "it's because they couldn't do it safely. By that I mean if I was killed in that hotel room the authorities would start looking for someone who might have known me in the past. I hadn't after all had time to meet anyone in Rembrandt let alone make enemies. If they started probing into my past they just may have found that someone living near Rembrandt went soldiering with me once upon a time."

"Able Sharpe."

"Exactly. So to keep that connection from being made Sally had to be sacrificed. Then the blame for that could fall on me and the law could take its course."

"You realize that that means Sheriff Flowers probably isn't in on this."

"How's that?"

"Simply that if they were afraid of the law making a connection during an investigation—well, Flowers would be the one investigating, wouldn't he? If they could buy him then there wouldn't have been any point in going about it the way they did."

"Maybe. There's still the business of the brand though."

"What do you mean?"

"He claimed he didn't recognize the Rafter CB brand."

"I can't explain that," Coral said. She was silent for a moment, just staring at the embers. "And what about Able Sharpe? It's true I've been away, but I never have heard of him. Never."

"He may not have been around long. Likely he's using an assumed name."

"Shelter—" she hesitated. "Why do you do this?"

"Do what?"

"Keep tracking these men down. It's been years now. One day they'll shoot first."

"I guess they will." He didn't answer her question. He would have had to tell her about those men who had frozen to death that winter, those who had starved. The Union papers he had gotten in prison reported it as if it were a triumph for their cause. Men had died screaming in agony because there was no medical help. And when they looked around for their officers they found them gone, run out with their pockets bulging with gold.

Why do it? How could he do otherwise?

Morning was hot, the sun a fierce yellow ball. Dry heat swept up off the desert. Shell, shirtless, worked in the shaft as Alejandro hauled the ore out in gunny sacks. Coral sat watch, squinting into the sunlight.

The next day was a repetition. Long hours in the airless shaft, shoulders and legs, back aching, going to sleep sweat-soaked and filthy, rising in four hours to stand watch, jumping at the call of an owl up the canyon, wondering if this time it was the Apaches.

It took a week before the high freight wagon was loaded and Shell was able to lean back, take a deep breath, feel that something had been achieved.

"I think," Alejandro cracked, "I have earn my dollar a day."

He was right. The Mexican hadn't shirked for a moment. As the days went by his attitude toward Shell had mellowed. They had worked side by side to fill that wagon with high grade ore, laboring in an airless shaft, their lungs clotted with dust. There had been no complaints from Alejandro.

"You've earned more than that," Coral told him. "You'll see, Alex, once we've really got the mine operating, you'll be repaid."

"Maybe you make me foreman when you have a big crew, eh?" Alex leaned back against the wagon, fanning himself with his sombrero. His beard was dark and wild, his chest streaked darkly with dirt.

"If you want it," Coral said responding seriously to his joke. "You can have that job." Coral looked at Shell and he saw disappointment there. He would not be here when that time came. He would be somewhere down the road hunting another man . . . or lying dead

131

out on the desert.

Shelter had said nothing about it, but Coral realized that this ride with her might be the last. If she was able to convert this load of ore into men and equipment she would have no need of him. No business need.

"Let's get 'em hitched," Shelter said and Alejandro, mopping his throat with a red bandana nodded.

The Percherons were backed in, looking sleek and strong. The lead team followed and was hitched, harness buckled, trace chains snapped into place.

"You'll have to drive, Coral," he told her. "Alejandro and I will work ahead of you, trying to clear some sort of road. The trail we used coming up was all right with an empty wagon, but it won't do for this load."

Coral nodded, following instructions dumbly. It really didn't seem to matter much somehow. He had mattered, but he was only a vagrant wind, touching her body before drifting away again.

"Coral?" Shell's voice brought her out of her reveries. "I asked if you were ready?"

"I'm ready," she answered, pulling on her gloves, unwinding the reins from the brake handle. Then she started the team into slow motion, the wagon tilting awkwardly as it crept forward with its great load.

It took an hour and a half, but they made it down. At three separate points Alejandro and Shell had had to tie on with lines to keep the wagon upright, and once for a terrifying moment the right hand wheels had come up off the ground as Shelter and Alejandro cursed, straining against the lines, and Coral's heart had stopped.

Yet the wagon had settled and they had reached the flats intact, heavily loaded with thousands of dollars in high grade gold ore.

Ahead lay Rembrandt, across that vast red desert. Rembrandt and a regular freighter's run to Posthill where the Triple X mines operated an ore crusher and refinery.

And ahead of Coral Scant a new life. Rich and uncertain, and as bleak as the desert itself. She shook off the mood. She had come back to Rembrandt with one purpose in mind, and by God, she was accomplishing that purpose! She, with the men's help, had beaten the long odds.

"Let's move it out, boys!" she shouted. "Rembrandt's ahead and with luck we'll be in by noon."

12.

"Sorry, Mister Brunner." The banker shook his head. "I'm going to have to call that note due. I owe it to the stockholders."

His name was Ambrose Peltier. He was fifty-nine years old, but with his pink, plump, almost cherubic face, folks generally guessed his age at ten to fifteen years less.

His expression now was gentle, kindly as he cut the props out from under one of his best customers. Peltier steepled his pudgy fingers and leaned back in his chair, looking across his desk at the horse rancher.

"You told me my line of credit was thirty thousand, Ambrose," Carl Brunner said. His badly scarred face twitched uncontrollably. Brunner's one good eye stared somberly, unhappily at the banker who shrugged.

"Times change, Mister Brunner."

"You led me to believe . . ."

"I led you to believe nothing, sir. Your account is no different than anyone else's. You have stretched your credit to the limit buying blood horses."

"Necessary in my business."

"It is also necessary to pay for them, Mister Brunner," Peltier said with some savagery.

"When the army purchase-order comes through, sir," Brunner said, leaning forward, "I shall be able to repay the loan in full, promptly, and you know it."

"No, sir. I don't know it."

Brunner nodded. He leaned back, touching his fingertips to his badly scarred face. It was his own fault, trusting this pink pig of a man. Since the accident his mind hadn't been that sharp. Still, he had thought he would always have the horse ranch. Now this fat little fart was threatening to take that from him. He smoothed back his white hair and tried again: "Mister Peltier, you know damn well I have signed a contract to provide the army with one hundred horses. You also realize that the Federal bureaucracy moves very slowly, but methodically. I can show you the contracts." Here Brunner fished into his pocket, his clawlike right hand searching for the papers which he had brought to the Rembrandt National Bank to offer as collateral, never believing that Peltier would crawfish on him.

"Sorry. The note is due, overdue, as you know, Mister Brunner."

"You encouraged me to borrow beyond my credit line!" Brunner said, coming half out of his chair, his old temper flaring up briefly.

"I did? This is most doubtful, Mister Brunner. As I have said, I owe it to my stockholders to call this note. I can give you a seven-day extension."

At that Carl Brunner threw back his white head and

laughed loudly until he fell into a coughing fit. Dabbing at his lips with his handkerchief he shook his head. "There's no point in that, Mister Peltier, is there? Where in hell can I come up with the money?" Without conscious thought Carl Brunner's head turned toward the big green safe in the corner of Peltier's office. Peltier seemed not to notice.

Walt Fogarty's head suddenly appeared in the half-open door to Peltier's office and Carl Brunner felt his mouth twist into a distasteful grimace. He had no use at all for Fogarty. The tall, blond gunman had worked for Brunner for three weeks until Jed had caught him stealing money from the cook's coffee tin and run him off. Sometime a week later a bullet had come within inches of killing Jed, a bullet fired from ambush as the old foreman was busy herding cattle out of an isolated arroyo.

"Mister Peltier?" Fogarty called. He spared a moment to grin derisively at Brunner.

"My, God," Brunner thought, "does everyone know what a tight spot I'm in?"

"What is it, Walt?"

"Private matter," Fogarty said and the banker rose as if with great weariness from behind his desk. With a last glance at Carl Brunner who looked older, smaller, whiter than ever, Peltier followed the thug out into the bank lobby.

"Yes?" Peltier hooked his thumbs in his vest pockets and nodded across the room to a depositor.

"She's comin' in. Little Joe Featherstone saw her with those two hired men."

"How . . . ! Has she got a wagon?"

"It looks like Brunner's big freight wagon, Mister

Peltier."

Peltier glanced back at his closed office door, his mouth pursing sourly. "All right. Do you have some people," Peltier asked, his voice dropping to a whisper.

"Enough for this."

"Then do it," Peltier hissed. "And make sure."

Fogarty looked wounded. Of course he would do it. Of course he would make sure. Didn't he always? Peltier watched the gunman saunter out of the bank, using the alley entrance. Then, his spirits brightening, he returned to the office where Carl Brunner sat waiting for the hammer to fall.

Shelter Morgan got down again, again removed the shovel from the hooks on the side of the freight wagon, again began digging beneath the wheels of the wagon which, again, had gotten itself mired in deep sand.

It was slow going, but none of them minded it. They were within sight of Rembrandt, and the threat of an Apache attack was minimal. The wagon was solid, the team sound, and there was a load of gold-bearing ore ready to be delivered. There was only a little impatience in them, no anger, no frustration as they cleared the wagon again, Alejandro working as fast, as diligently as Shell.

"Pull it!" Shell barked and Coral snapped the reins, the big team starting the ore wagon into motion once more. Shell and Alejandro stood leaning on their shovels for a minute, catching their breath.

"From here it is a breeze," Alejandro said, looking down the slope toward Rembrandt. The sand grew shallow as the rising hills formed windbreaks. Half a mile on the road was rocky rather than sandy, and another half mile would see them into Rembrandt. "Last time I need this shovel, hombre!" Alejandro laughed, throwing it away.

He was right. The bullet slammed into his chest and he cartwheeled him backward as Shell lunged for the reins of his sorrel, palming his Colt simultaneously.

A dozen more shots rang out from the hills as Shell grabbed Alejandro by his belt and dragged him toward the pile of rocks to the south of the trail, his pistol throwing up a covering blanket of hot lead.

Behind the rocks he reloaded, his eyes sweeping the hills, seeing no targets. What he did see turned his blood cold. The team, stampeded by the gunshots, was racing wildly down the slope and the brake, Coral's frantic tugging on the reins, was doing nothing at all to slow it. With the weight of that ore behind it, it was running wild toward oblivion.

Alejandro's eyes were wide, white. His hands were clasped on his chest, crimson blood seeping through the interlocked fingers. Blood frothed from his lips. He was going and going fast, and he knew it.

"Get out. Run," he said through the blood which filled his mouth. Shots racketed down the canyon and Shelter ducked low, his head next to Alejandro's.

"They'll not come down, Alejandro. Not while we're behind these rocks. Hold tight. It's only a mile to town and a doctor."

"Might as well be a hundred miles, amigo," Alejandro said.

Shell lifted up, fired three shots at the hidden guns on the hill and ducked again. Alejandro was smiling, his dark eyes unnaturally bright.

"You weren't such a bastard, Shelter Morgan."

138

"Nor were you, Alejandro Orta," Shelter said softly. But Alejandro never heard it. He was dead and Shelter cursed violently. He raised up, emptied his Colt and reloaded. Crawling downslope away from the road he saw what he had feared. Coral had lost control of the team and as Shelter watched, his muscles taut, eyes narrowed to slits, a bile rising in his throat, he saw her leap free, saw the wagon begin to roll, scattering ore everywhere as the horses raced frantically across the flats.

The snipers opened up again and Shell had to belly down, pressing his face to the heated sand. They kept him pinned down for nearly an hour. He couldn't even lift his head to see if Coral was alive or dead, if she lay crippled against the stony earth.

The sun rose to its sweltering zenith and then began to slowly slip toward the horizon and still Shelter did not dare move. They were up there somewhere, waiting.

He felt rather than heard the thunder of the horses as they galloped toward him. He chanced lifting his head and saw two dozen men on horseback riding out from Rembrandt.

The man in the lead was Sheriff Flowers.

He saw them pull up saw them dismount and rush to where Coral lay and his breath caught. Someone picked her up and she was limp in his arms. But she was alive! He could tell that by the gentleness with which they handled her, placed her down on a blanket. He could see nothing else.

The posse split then, half of them starting upslope, and Morgan took off down the rock-strewn, cactus-stippled slope toward the dry watercourse blow, slipping, sliding, falling, tearing his hands and knees, elbows.

Shell dropped over a searing gray granite ledge, dropping to the bottom of the dry creek bed just as the posse riding past spotted Alejandro.

"Someone down there," he heard a voice call.

"Be careful, Tom."

"No need to be careful with this one," the deputy answered grimly.

There were further shouts, much grumbling, cursing and stomping around.

"Anybody up there?"

Shelter again lifted his head. Three deputies that he could see sat their horses on the stony ridge above the trail.

"Not now, but there's casings all over the place. Looks like Bull Run up here."

"All right, come on down!" In a lower voice the deputy speculated, "Looks like the gang of them hit the lady from up there. The Mex must have been with her. We'll have to wait until she can talk to find out more, I guess."

Until she can talk! Shelter felt his gut tighten. He could not see Coral from where he now hid, Colt in hand, but when he had last seen her she was still, unmoving. Unconscious . . . or worse. At least he knew she was alive.

That was hardly enough to still the anger rising in Shelter Morgan. Someone had hurt that small, dark-eyed girl, tried to kill her. And they would pay. All other thoughts drifted out of Shelter's mind. There was only vengeance left. Cold, steely vengeance. They would pay.

He waited another hour until the posse had returned to town, carrying Coral and Alejandro's body with them. Then, chilled, stiff, still angry, he crawled out of the gorge.

He moved cautiously upslope, eyes flickering to each shadow. He reached the trail and stood there breathing deeply, looking around him.

The wagon had been smashed to kindling. The ore was scattered across the hillside. Most of it had fallen down into the gorge itself. It could be recovered—with a deal of work. But there was no wagon now—Brunner would have to be repaid for that. There were no laborers. Both had been killed.

And the mine owner—he preferred not to think of that. Coral was injured, perhaps badly, and Shelter couldn't do a damn thing to help her. Anything but find the killers.

He climbed the hill above the trail, sweat raining off him although the breeze out of the west was cool as the sun declined.

It was as the deputy had said, reminiscent of a full-scale battle up there. Brass cartridge casings littered the hillside where the ambushers had concealed themselves.

Shelter stood there holding a single casing, eyes searching the ground. Then he threw the casing down angrily. What was he going to do, run them down afoot?

The sheriff had split his party. Half the posse had ridden out after the ambushers, heading southward. Climbing to the crest of the hill Shell looked out across the desert. Far to the distant south he could see what might have been men on horseback riding toward

Mexico.

He frowned, his eyes narrowing. He turned and looked back across the low-growing manzanita and sage toward Rembrandt. Then he smiled faintly, turning to walk back down the hillslope.

Those men weren't headed for Mexico. They weren't bandits on the run, but men sent out to do a particular job. They would ride south until they had eluded the posse, then they would turn and ride home. Home to Rembrandt.

And Shelter Morgan would be waiting.

He slipped into town under cover of night. There was still a faint pinkish bank of light above the western mountains, a single star brilliantly piercing the vague wash of color. Uptown the saloon was open, by the sound of it a few of the locals had had enough time to get themselves tanked up.

Shelter walked through the alleys, keeping to the shadows, working his way uptown.

He stopped suddenly and pressed himself to the wall of the saddlery behind him. Three men were approaching, all swaying a little as they walked. Their voices came to him clearly.

". . . Coral Scant. She's back and someone shot her."

"Shot a woman!"

"Yes, and that's not half of it. She was comin' into town with a load of gold ore—high grade stuff, Ed Graves said, and he ought to know, he was up there. It's just scattered all over the hillside up there."

"She's found her old man's mine."

"Found it and is workin' it. Was workin' it."

"Where's she now?"

142

"Hotel. Doc Vaughn was over there. Didn't say a word about her chances."

"Damn me," one of them breathed. "And a mountain of gold sittin' out there all lonely."

They passed by and Shelter stood scowling in the darkness. It had begun. Coral was down hurt, the mine unguarded. The vultures would begin flocking.

He had learned something useful, however. Coral was in the hotel. From what the men had said, he took it that it was serious. The doctor had made no comment. If it had been nothing but a bump on the head, Shell guessed the doctor wouldn't have been so reticent about talking, at least that had been his experience where the medical profession was concerned.

Orienting himself he moved through the alleys toward the hotel, an uneasiness thumping in his chest. If she died . . . he gave it no more thought, banishing it from his mind. Shell crept up toward the hotel, seeing his own room, the room where Sally had been murdered.

There had been more than one woman hurt on Shell's account. At times he wondered if he had the right to involve them in his life.

Two windows were lighted and he eased up to the first, removing his hat as he peered in. It was a delightful sight—or would have been at another time. A tall redheaded woman was sitting half-dressed on the bed, arms raised as she stretched. Shell ducked and continued on. The second room he came to was Coral's.

He heard low voices, women's voices, saw the nurse walking toward the door, shaking her head.

". . . to me neither. Poor little thing. She's still got

that fever too."

"Plain out of her head," another sympathetic voice said. Shell saw a woman in a dark dress furiously knitting, sitting in a corner chair.

"She'll be all right," the other woman said, but there was no conviction, only a vague hope in her voice.

Shelter shifted his position and now he was able to see Coral. Her face was waxen, like someone who's been laid out for the funeral. Her hands were even clasped on her stomach. She barely moved, barely breathed. Her dark hair was loose; someone had brushed it out. There was a big purple bruise on her right arm, a laceration on her head just at the hairline.

Shelter turned away, squatting down in the shadows, feeling sick and angry. She was living yet, and that was some comfort, but not much.

He stood, taking in deep breaths. The night had grown cold. The town was silent but for the constant, forced hilarity in the saloon up the street. Shelter Morgan checked his guns and settled in to wait.

13.

Midnight came and went. Shelter Morgan sat shivering in the alley beside the stable. He had seen no one but the Mexican who ran the stable. He had appropriated an empty rain barrel to use as a seat. There he perched, rifle across his lap, watching the main street of Rembrandt. Watching and waiting—and how much time had he spent doing that these past dozen years?

It was as much a part of a warrior's life to wait as it was to fling yourself upon the enemy. Shelter had spent much time waiting and he was good at it.

Now he sat there, eyes cold and dark, mouth set, the terrible anger barely under control. A gang of men had set upon a single woman, trying to kill her. Someone had coldly calculated that. Sat down and planned it out.

And that someone was, had to be, the man who was responsible for the death of Paco, for the death of Aaron Scant himself. Gold, or the promise of it, had driven someone over the edge of sanity, creating an animal out of what was meant to be a man.

Shell stiffened, stood, pressed himself into the shadows. There were horsemen coming up the street. Their mounts were dragging, that was obvious by their pace. Shell waited, his pulse thudding in his ears, the cool weight of the Winchester in his hands.

". . . sleep."

"Yeah, well we'd better talk to Flowers first."

"What the hell for? He's sleeping, ain't he!"

It was the posse dragging in. Their horses were coated with salt and dust. The men were slumped in their saddles. They had no prisoners with them.

"Let him ride down to the border if he wants. To hell with them badlands."

They rode past at a shuffle, grumbling and cursing. Shell watched them approach the sheriff's office and swing down, standing sullenly as one man banged on the door. There was no answer, and after another minute of complaining, the men dispersed, heading home to bed.

Shelter watched them go and then settled in again, pulling his collar up, hunching his shoulders. It would be a long cold night. The stars slowly shifted and Rembrandt fell silent as a ghost town. A wandering skunk was the only living thing Shell saw for hours. It waddled down the alley, scavenging, and seemed not to recognize Shell as a living thing, certainly it didn't feel threatened. He watched it with amusement.

Suddenly the amusement was wiped from his face. The skunk took off up the alley. Shelter stood, listening intently. Horses coming in. He wiped his hand on his pants and gripped the rifle more tightly.

He worked his way to the head of the alley and

peered out, bathed in shadows. Two riders coming in. Both lean, both riding exhausted horses. Shell watched them as they neared the stable.

"Kick the damn door in," one of them shouted.

"Hey, Pedro!"

After a minute the Mexican appeared, sleepy-eyed. The men went inside, and by the faint glow of Pedro's lantern Shell studied their faces, committing them to memory. But he did not move. Half an hour later the men, each with a bedroll over his shoulder emerged from the stable. The older man had a cigarette hanging from his lips.

". . . hell, no. That's Fogarty's affair. Me, I'm going to sleep."

They walked away, their boots crunching gravel. Fogarty. It meant nothing to Shelter, but they had acted as if Fogarty were boss man.

Shell settled in again, pitying Pedro who had turned out his lamp and gone to bed again. An hour later two more men trailed in. Slowly filtering into Rembrandt, they walked boldly down the main street. Two men now, two more later perhaps. A single man entering from the south of town, two from the north.

They had led the posse on a merry chase onto the desert, split up and now, singly and in pairs, they had returned to Rembrandt.

"Shut up. You'll get paid," Shelter heard one of this pair say.

"Listen, Fogarty . . ."

"You listen, ass-face, you'll have yours when I get mine."

The other man, apparently intimidated by Fogarty, fell silent. Shell tensed as they too approached the stable. Fogarty sat his horse as the other man swung down. Shelter studied the badman, seeing a tall, blond man wearing a new, if dusty black hat tugged low. It was decorated with silver conchoes on the hatband. He wore a silver-mounted Colt hung low, and the insolent, brassy expression of a man who knew he was better than the rest with a gun.

He was a type Shelter knew well. You found them in saloons, sitting beside a warring cattleman, waiting for the chance to use their guns, wanting to show how good they are wanting to stand over a bloody victim, to turn away, smiling.

Shelter knew Walt Fogarty without ever having seen him before. Knew him for what he was. And he knew that they would face one another before this was over.

There he was, smiling, rolling a ciqarette—and across the street Coral Scant lay near death in a hotel bed. Shell tried to swallow and found his throat too constricted.

"You going over, Fogarty?"

"Yeah. I'll see the man."

"Okay. Walt, you got two dollars for a bottle?" the other gunhand asked.

"Not feeling so good, Baker!" Fogarty laughed.

"Not so good," Baker answered and Fogarty fished two silver dollars from his tight jeans pocket and dropped them on the earth before turning his horse and riding it away. Baker stood staring after him for half a minute before he crouched and searched frantically for the dollars.

He found the first dollar and pocketed it quickly. Turning, studying the ground intently, he spotted the second and was reaching out for it with relief when the boot covered it.

Baker stood frozen with cold apprehension. He slowly lifted his eyes to see the tall dark-haired man in the torn shirt standing over him, rifle in hands.

"My dollar, mister," Baker tried.

"Is it? How'd you earn it, Baker?"

"Who the hell are you!" Baker came up angrily, reaching for his gun. The butt of the Winchester arced up and slammed into his chin, splitting it wide. Baker sprawled back, bleeding from the face, his head ringing. The tall man stood over him.

"What do you want?" the gunman asked shakily.

"I asked you what you did for two silver dollars, Baker?" The voice was cold, steely.

"I just . . . hell," he said miserably, "I guess you know."

"That's right. I know, Baker," Shelter Morgan said.

Baker swallowed hard. For a minute Shell thought he was going to draw his belt gun. His fingers twitched and the tendons on his neck stood out tautly. Then the sand ran out of him and he just sat there nodding.

"All right," he said, "What is it?"

"I want to see the boss," Shell told him. Deftly he reached across and slid Baker's pistol from his holster.

"All right. You take the creek road . . ."

"No chance. You're taking me."

"Me! If they see me doing that, they'll kill me."

"Maybe. I'll do it for sure if you don't," Morgan said, and Baker swallowed hard again, looking deep into those icy eyes. He nodded.

"All right. I'll get my horse," he said, rising.

149

"We'll do it together," Shell said.

Baker turned and swung open the stable door. Pedro roused again from his sleep lit the lantern and emerged from his nook, eyes scowling. Then they opened wide. He saw Baker and the tall man behind him, gun jammed into the bandit's back.

"Morgan!" Pedro said in astonishment.

"Need a horse, Pedro."

"Take whatever you want," he said, backing away, the lantern at knee height. The stablehand stood gawking at the man the whole country was looking for, the murderer, Shelter Morgan.

"Saddle up for me too, will you, Baker?" Shell asked amiably.

"Sure," Baker said, trying to sound surly, managing only to sound badly frightened, as he was.

"Which one, Pedro?"

"The gray is very fast, señor," the stablehand said.

"All right. The gray, Baker. I'll bring him back and settle up when I have the time, Pedro."

The stablehand didn't answer. His knees were wobbling. He was wondering if he was going to catch a bullet in the next few minutes, if he was living out the last few moments of his life.

"I'd go back to bed, Pedro," Shell advised him. "I'd go to sleep and count this all as a dream."

"Yes."

"Do you understand me?"

"I will tell no one."

"I wouldn't want to find anyone on my back trail, Pedro. I'll know who tipped them. If that happens I'll be back."

"I understand."

150

"Good." Baker had saddled his own horse and the stable gray. Now he stepped into leather, still watching Shell. Morgan swung up, keeping his Colt on Baker as he did so. He shucked the rifle from Baker's saddle boot and slid it into his own. Holstering his pistol he rode up on Baker's right side, keeping his own rifle on the bandit as he told him, "Move out now. And let's take it easy until we get to know one another. Understand?"

Baker understood all right, but he couldn't answer with his mouth dry and cottony like it was. He nodded agreement and started forward, Shell speaking softly across his shoulder to the stablehand.

"Good night, Pedro."

Then they were out into the main street, slowly walking their horses westward toward the creek. It was cooler yet, damp when they reached it. Cattails grew thickly for a distance, the frogs grumbling in their hidden haunts. The crickets fell silent as the riders passed, Baker's face pale in the starlight.

"Look, Morgan . . ."

"Shut up. You ride with me or you stay here. Face down."

They went on silently, climbing into a row of grassy hills, following a road well worn by wagon wheels. Abruptly the spreading white house came into view. A lamp burned in one window.

"That's it," Baker said.

"Who owns the house?"

Shell's horse shifted its feet. It was a second before Baker answered with an exasperated sigh. "Ambrose Peltier. The town banker."

"He's the one who paid for this job?"

"I figured he was. Fogarty didn't say, but he was always hanging around Peltier, doing things for him. Yeah, it's Peltier you want."

"Turn around," Shell said. Baker hesitated and he added, "That's the easy way, Baker."

He nodded and turned and Shell clubbed him behind the ear with his rifle butt. Baker sagged to the ground, his horse shying away.

Morgan got down and bound Baker hand and foot using Baker's belt and shirt. Then he stuffed his scarf into his mouth and rolled him off into the brush.

Stepping back into the saddle he kneed the gray forward, hoping that it was a runner as Pedro had claimed. He might have cause to test it this night.

The house was silent, dark but for the single window which faintly glowed, casting cross-hatched patterns on the earth. There were no guards that Shelter saw. A single horse was ground-hitched beside the house where a back door led in through a narrow porch.

Shell slipped from the gray, leaving his rifle. It would be close-in work if there was any shooting, and it was shooting he planned on.

He sifted through the shadows cast by the huge overhanging oaks, and reached the small porch without a shout being raised.

Shell palmed the brass doorknob and turned. The door swung open on oiled hinges and Morgan stepped inside the house. He paused, searching the darkened interior of the kitchen where he found himself.

From somewhere to his left he heard a voice raised briefly, and he crept across the kitchen floor. A side door, standing open, let out into a carpeted hallway.

152

Two doors on Shell could see a yellow ribbon of light.

Holding his Colt, barrel up, beside his ear he walked that way, his boots whispering against the carpet.

"What about Brunner?" the voice of Walt Fogarty asked.

"Don't worry about him. The old man is broken. He'll be too busy scrambling to pay off his note to involve himself in the girl's business."

"If she lives."

"Yes, that may have been a mistake. People won't like it if she dies."

"Hell, Mister Peltier, the wagon rolled. Nobody shot at her."

"It doesn't matter." Shell stiffened at the casual way they dismissed Coral, her life or death. "She's got no one to watch that claim, does she? No one else?"

"Both the Mexicans are dead. There's that tall man, but that's all. One man don't count for much anyway."

"Good." The satisfaction in the banker's voice was infuriating. Shell's hand stretched out and touched the doorknob to Peltier's study. "We've got that claim. We spent enough damn time looking for it. As soon as I found out the girl was coming back, I knew we'd get it. Rich, Fogarty, that mine is rich. Old Aaron Scant showed me some of his samples the day he came begging for a loan. I turned him down, of course, figuring he'd have to give it up. But that damned Brunner loaned him money, kept him alive."

"Temporarily," Fogarty said with enjoyment.

"That," the strange voice said from the doorway, "is an apt word, gentlemen. You are alive as well. But

153

it is only temporarily."

"You!" Peltier jerked in his chair, his pink hands rigidly clenching the arms. His eyes bugged out of his head. He looked steadily at the tall man silhouetted in his doorway, gawked at the big blue Colt in his hand.

Walt Fogarty was a different matter. The gunman's eyes were cool, his manner relaxed as he sat opposite Peltier studying Shelter Morgan.

"Thought I'd gotten rid of you," Fogarty said. Then, uncrossing his legs casually, he kicked out with his boot, sending the kerosene lamp beside him crashing to the floor, plunging the room into darkness as the guns opened up.

14.

Peltier had been the first to fire. As Fogarty made his move the banker's hand dipped inside of his coat and came up filled with a little Colt.41. He swung onto his target, pulling the trigger frantically as the lamp hit the floor and burst into flames.

Peltier's bullet slammed into the door sill beside Shelter's head and he ducked reflexively, firing back at the banker. Shell's bullet ripped through Peltier's shoulder below the collar bone and penetrated deep into the stuffing of the chair back behind him. The banker screamed with pain.

Shell immediately turned his attention and his gun-sights on Walt Fogarty. The gunman had rolled from his chair and had come to one knee, bringing his pistol level. The flames from the seeping kerosene back-lighted him weirdly as he squeezed off two rapid shots at Morgan.

Shell was already moving, however, diving behind a plush settee as Fogarty's shots whined past him, tearing holes in the pale plaster wall beyond Shelter Morgan.

Shell popped up, threw a snap shot at Fogarty, had a quick glance at Peltier who was sagged in his chair, clenching his shattered shoulder, and was met by an answering bullet from Fogarty.

Fogarty fired again and then broke for the window, holding his arm up before his face as a shield against the flames which had caught the draperies now and were climbing the walls. Peltier bellowed with pain and fear. Morgan touched off as Fogarty reached the window. The big .44 slug shattered spine and muscles and the gunman lurched forward, crashing headfirst through the window to lie hanging half in, half out of the room.

The draft from the window caught the flames and they roared into life, climbing the walls to lick at the ceiling, their crackling loud in Shelter's ears. Peltier screamed again with anguish and Shelter started that way though the flames snatched at his body and the smoke from the kerosene fire was thick and black.

"Peltier!"

"No!" the banker cried shrilly. He had seen Fogarty go down and now he was certain Morgan meant to kill him as well. He bounded from his chair and crossed the room toward the window, his right arm dragging.

"Come back here, you fool!" Shell cried, but Peltier never heard him above the roar of the flames. Shell had to back out of the room which was alive with dancing, crackling flame now.

He caught a last glimpse of Peltier, his coat afire, then heard the crash which might have been Peltier falling to the floor. The flames engulfed the room now,

156

creeping across the ceiling and Morgan burst out into the smoke filled hallway.

Right into the sights of the two men who had rushed downstairs still in longjohns.

The man in front had a rifle and as he took it to his shoulder, Shelter firing from his hip punched him back with a chest shot. The guard's arms were out-flung, his face twisted with pain as he went down. Shell shifted his muzzle to the second guard, a kid of no more than seventeen or eighteen. His mouth was hanging open as he looked from his dead partner to the roaring tongues of flame flickering out of the bank-er's study to the tall, hard man with the Colt.

"What's it going to be, kid?" Shell asked angrily. "I haven't got all night."

The kid threw down his gun and took to his heels. Shell turned in the opposite direction, heading for the front door of Peltier's house. He was out the front door and into the yard before he heard the rumbling sound, the great creaking groan and turned in time to see a section of Peltier's roof cave in, great golden sparks gouting high into the night sky.

Shelter watched for one long minute then turned and headed back toward where the gray had been tied.

Morgan rode to where Baker lay in a sweat, ex-hausted after trying to free himself from his bonds, and he stepped down to walk to where the badman lay.

With his knife Shell slit the shirt and belt he had used to tie Baker. The man sat up, rubbing his wrists and ankles, his face glistening with perspiration. Baker frowned and looked northward, seeing the dis-tant glow of fire.

"What's that?" Baker asked.

"Looks like you won't be getting paid," Shell told him. Baker nodded, looking decidedly unhappy.

"What's going to happen to me?"

"That's completely up to you," Shell said. "Get on that horse, point it east and don't ever look back, and nothing else will happen. Hang around Rembrandt and the next time I see you, I'll kill you on sight."

"Like that, is it?"

"It's just like that."

"Which way's east?"

Baker got into leather and whipped his horse out of there, probably half-expecting a bullet in the back at any moment. Shelter stood watching him go. Then he watched the glow of the distant fire burning itself out against the night-darkened land.

He felt no pride, no satisfaction, no relief. Only a sense of a duty done. They were the ones who had wanted to shoot it out. They were the ones who had tried to run a young woman off her claim and steal it for themselves. They were the ones who had killed Aaron Scant, Alejandro and Paco. He felt no guilt at all, yet there was no pride to be taken in such a night's work.

Shelter stepped into the stirrup and swung aboard the gray, turning back toward Rembrandt, needing to know how Coral was, if she would make it through the long, dark and blood-stained night.

He hit Rembrandt two hours before dawn, leaving the gray in the willows along the creek as he walked into town, alert for any sign of Flowers or his deputies. Apparently they were all sound asleep after a long day's chase across the desert. The town was a ghost

158

town as Shelter slipped through the alleys and walked into the hotel.

The clerk was behind the desk, sleeping, arms folded, a fluttering snore escaping his lips. Shell walked on by him.

He found Coral's room and after listening, went in. No one was there. Just Coral, small, fragile, pale. Morgan took off his hat and sat in the chair beside her. Almost immediately her eyes popped open.

"Thought so," she said in a far away voice. "Thought you were around, you maverick."

Then her eyes closed again, but her hand stretched out, cool and white and Shell took it in his own broad brown hand. He sat with her for half an hour, watching the rise and fall of her breast, the tension in her face as she fought against the battering her body had taken.

Later on she came around again. "Oh, hello, Shell," she said with surprise. "When did you come in?"

"A while ago. Ready to go home?"

"Not just yet," she said weakly. "The gold!"

"All taken care of." He kissed her hand and said, "We collected it all. Everything's fine."

"You and Alejandro?"

"Yes. We collected the gold."

"And Father's watching the mine?"

"That's right," Shell told her, feeling his heart drop. "He's watching it."

"The Apaches . . ."

"That's all taken care of. Your father made peace talk with them."

"They always respected him." Her head rolled and she looked at Shell, through him, her hand tightening on his. "What about Carl's wagon?"

"Oh, that. He came on over and we talked about it. There's enough ore to buy him an even better one."

"He's a good man. And very handsome—you'd better watch out, Shelter Morgan," she said weakly.

"Handsome?" Shell couldn't keep the astonishment out of his voice. Carl Brunner was white-haired, one-eyed, scarred and old. Unless Coral had some very strange prejudices, the description didn't match at all.

"Coral?" He squeezed her hand. "What does Carl Brunner look like?"

"Tall," she said sleepily, "not so tall as you. Dark haired, with shining dark eyes. Amused eyes. Strong capable hands." She seemed to fall asleep, but she added, "Not so pretty as you, Mister Morgan, if that's what's worrying you."

"Yes, Coral, that's what was worrying me. I want you all for myself. And when you're well . . ." but she had fallen off again and Shelter dropped into silence. After another minute he rose, bent low to kiss her forehead right where the savage laceration began, then turned and walked out the door, passing a startled looking nurse whose mouth dropped open to ask a question she never voiced.

Shelter went out through the lobby, past the still sleeping, still snoring clerk. After a careful glance up and down the main street he walked out and turned upstreet, his mind tumbling with questions.

Coral's description, damnit, matched that of Able Sharpe. Yet from what he had heard other places, Carl Brunner was white-haired, one-eyed, stooped.

It hit him suddenly. No one was lying. Something had happened. Something in the three-year interval between the time Coral had last seen Carl Brunner and now. Something which had destroyed Carl Brunner's face and health. But what?

Shelter had started back toward the river, wanting to ride the gray well away from town and find a place to hole up through the daylight hours. He was half a block from the bank when the explosion was touched off.

His head jerked around and he saw the bank tremble as if shaking in massive, invisible hands. Smoke curled out of a back window. Uptown a door burst open, a voice cried out. Behind Shelter the sheriff's office came to life. A lantern was lighted, a door thrown open. Flowers himself emerged in minutes, dashing upstreet, shirtless, rifle in his hand.

Morgan ducked into the nearest alley, seeing simultaneously the side door to Peltier's bank bang open and a man struggling under the weight of two heavy sacks make his way to a waiting black horse.

"Hey, you! Halt!" Flowers shouted. Shelter didn't wait to discover if the sheriff was calling to him or the bank robber. He ran down the alley, stumbling over a litter of tin cans beside the restaurant, and emerged behind the bank, watching the bank robber swing into leather and head out toward the river, the black horse running smoothly as Sheriff Flowers' rifle barked.

Shell had a good look at him. Too good. A hunched man with white hair and a black patch over one eye. Carl Brunner had just blown the Rembrandt National Bank's safe and was now making a clean getaway with most of its assets.

Carl Brunner. Able Sharpe.

The town was alive with shouting now, lanterns

161

flickered everywhere like fireflies darting madly about. Shell decided Rembrandt was no place to stay healthy just now and he hot-footed it toward the creek.

Brunner had a good start. It was doubtful the posse, by the time it could be formed, would ever catch Brunner.

Shelter Morgan meant to.

He was onto the gray's back and away through the willows toward the broken hills beyond before the sun rose on Rembrandt and the sheriff standing before the dynamited safe could scratch his head and slowly, profusely curse.

"Someone better ride out to Mister Peltier's house and tell him he's got some trouble," Flowers said.

The sheriff was wrong. Peltier had no further problems. He never would again.

Morgan rode slowly toward the Rafter CB, the rising sun warm on his back. His senses were alert to possible danger along the trail, but his mind roamed through a labyrinth of fuzzy, seemingly unconnected thoughts, trying to make some order out of the night's events.

Coral Scant's father had found a rich claim after years of searching these hills. But Aaron Scant never lived to cash in on his discovery. Someone, probably Walt Fogarty, had murdered him, mutilating him in order to throw suspicion on the Apaches. Why had he been murdered?

Apparently Scant had gone to the local banker to ask for a loan to develop the claim. But Ambrose Peltier, seeing the promise in those ore samples Scant produced, had gotten greedy and decided to take it all for himself. Fogarty was dispatched to kill the old man.

Meanwhile Scant had turned to Carl Brunner—Able Sharpe—who loaned Scant enough to get along on, probably because Brunner was in love with, or set on having Coral Scant.

With Scant's murder accomplished, Peltier had planned on moving in, buying out Coral, probably. But Coral had not only left Rembrandt, she had caved in a hillside over the claim, hiding it from any searchers, taking the secret with her to Indiana.

Peltier had had her watched and when after three years Coral had decided to come home, the banker had ordered the stage hit. Probably they meant to take Coral and demand the location of the mine. Maybe they would have forced her to sign over the claim.

But coincidence had intervened. Shelter Morgan was on that stage and he had held off the claim jumpers. Until yesterday.

Likely Fogarty had been in the hills keeping an eye on things and had seen the claim opened up again. He had also seen that Coral had recruited three fighting men. He had eliminated Paco immediately. Probably Paco had simply been in the wrong place at the wrong time. Fogarty, probing the canyon to see what progress Coral was making had more than likely simply stumbled on Paco and been forced to eliminate him, again trying to blame it on the Apaches.

Fine. Coral then actually got a load of ore ready for the mills and Peltier began to panic. He had to strike again and hard, knowing that with a few thousand dollars Coral could hire all the men and equipment she needed to effectively work the mine and keep poachers off the claim.

So he had hit, hard. The ambush had utilized

Fogarty's skills again. Alejandro had been killed, Coral injured seriously. Only Morgan was around to fight for the claim.

Apparently. But then Carl Brunner had made his move. Shell couldn't know about Peltier's entrapment and snubbing of Brunner, of his threat to foreclose on the note Brunner had signed, so the reason for Brunner's next move escaped him.

But he knew that Brunner had sneaked into Rembrandt on this night and had blown Peltier's safe. Very efficiently, with the skill of an experienced man.

That thought pulled Shelter up short. He halted the gray and sat on the breezy grassless knoll, remembering. Remembering the so-called Tucson Gang. The Tucson Gang which made a specialty of safe cracking. They had struck at banks across Arizona, twice halted trains to blow their safes until George C. McDonnel of the Arizona Eastern had laid a trap for the Tucson Gang.

Letting the word leak out that his railroad was carrying a hundred thousand in bullion, he had himself fixed the safe in the baggage car with fifty pounds of dynamite. When the Tucson gang tried to blow it with their own charge the safe had gone up with force enough to kill three of them.— And force enough to scar and blind a man.

15.

It was nearly noon before Shelter, picking his way through the broken ground had worked his way up on the north side of the Rafter CB ranch and was able to look down on the narrow valley which sheltered that herd of sleek blooded horses, the shorthorn cattle, the fine house of Carl Brunner.

He had come a long way and covered his tracks well, but the past comes home. It can come home with a bang. Able Sharpe's past was about to do just that.

Shelter dismounted and got to his belly, taking a long look at the set-up. He could see three or four men near the corral. Jed, the foreman, might have been one of them although it was hard to tell. Harold he saw. The kid was just east of Shell. Whatever he was supposed to be doing, he wasn't. He was just standing in the shade of an oak loosely holding the reins to his pinto pony, staring at the magnificent horse herd. Maybe he was dreaming of the day he'd have his own herd. Wondering how in the world a man ever came up with enough money to start a ranch like Rafter CB.

"The answer's easy," Shelter said under his breath. As easy as murder. All you do is start shooting at your own side. Kill them all then take the gold and run. Run like hell.

But you won't be able to run far enough and fast enough, Harold. No one can. The past comes home.

Shelter thought about brazening it out, riding down as Bob Winslow, Coral Scant's cousin, to explain about the freight wagon. But Able Sharpe was no fool. He must have figured it all out, figured who the tall stranger with the cold blue eyes was.

No, it was best to go in silently. He would have preferred the cover of darkness—getting back out wasn't going to be that easy, and he hated the idea of getting into a gunfight with a bunch of men who were only trying to earn a buck as working cowhands. Like Jed.

The cards would have to fall where they may, however, Shell was going in one way or the other. Where would Able Sharpe be at this hour? Sleeping after a hard night's work blowing the Rembrandt National's safe? Not likely. Breakfast then. Relaxing in the library, counting his money?

Shell stepped into leather and eased the gray down the long slope, keeping to the low ground. Emerging from the gully he found himself fifty yards from the shelter of the oak grove. Once into the trees there would be no problem reaching the house. Or so he hoped.

Looking around first, Shell casually started his horse forward, walking it. If spotted he would try to bluff it out as Bob Winslow, any undue haste or furtiveness would blow the chance of doing that.

He held his breath without realizing it until he was into the oaks, the horse crushing fallen leaves underfoot as

Morgan wove his way toward the big white house.

His eyes were moving constantly, his nerve endings tingling. From the shade of the trees he saw what he wanted. There was an upstairs window open. The dry breeze toyed with the curtains. Shell smiled thinly and dismounted, leaving the gray in the oaks as he moved across the open space toward the house.

Looking upward he saw that the house had a ledge between the two stories. He put a boot on the window-sill before him, stretched up and caught the ledge. Then soundlessly he pulled himself up and over, working along the eighteen-inch wide ledge toward the open window.

He swore he heard someone humming inside. Morgan eased up, his Colt in hand, stepped through the open window and found himself facing Able Sharpe.

"I've been expecting you."

Sharpe was at the mirror, trying to tie a scarf with one good hand, one which was badly crippled. He lifted his gaze to Shell and Morgan, looking into that scarred face could see only a shadow of the man he had been pursuing all these years. Sharpe turned toward him, his hands empty.

"You going to kill me?" he asked.

"No. Not like this. I'm not that kind."

"No," Sharpe shook his head, "I didn't think you were, Captain Morgan. What then?"

"I could take you in for the Rembrandt National robbery. By the time they let you out of jail, it wouldn't matter any more."

"You know about that?" Sharpe chuckled, crossing the room to sit on his bed, hands folded, his single eye gleaming with amusement. "You missed your calling,

Captain Morgan. You should have been a lawman."

"I am. Of sorts."

"Yes. Of sorts. I do get the newspapers. I've read about General Custis and Colonel Fainer. Poor Leland Mason and Reg Bowlen—yes, I knew you'd be here sooner or later."

"But you stayed."

"Yes. What's the point in running? If I leave the Rafter CB I have nothing. Besides, I am too old to run. Suddenly too old."

"You ought to have laid off that dynamite, Sharpe, you would have held together a little longer."

Sharpe laughed out loud. "You know about that too, do you? Rotten trick that was, loading that safe with explosives." The smile fell away from Sharpe's face. "How is Coral, Captain Morgan?"

"Not well. It's pretty bad."

"Damn," he said with genuine sorrow. "I liked that girl. I liked her very much. Asked her to marry me, you know—before my accident. It's Peltier, you know who's done this to her."

"I know."

Sharpe's eyebrow lifted. "Yes, I should have known. You're quite thorough. Been to see him?"

"I have."

Sharpe sucked thoughtfully at his lip, seeming to ignore the muzzle of the big blue Colt which was trained on him. "He wanted to foreclose on this ranch, Morgan. The bastard. I decided to get the money I needed. From his bank! Teach the little shit a lesson. He never learned it—you got him?"

"I got him."

"I thought so. And now me?"

"That was the idea."

"But not in cold blood."

"It's never been my way, Sharpe. I'm not like you bastards. You who murdered your own kind."

"You know, you're right. I always regretted that, Captain. I still think of it often. But I was young, knew the end of the war would find me broke. Knew the Yankees would take my land—that they hadn't cleared with fire." He puffed out his cheeks and blew. "I was young. It seemed expedient. Christ, everyone else was in on it. Colonel Fainer never really thought you'd fight when it came down to it. He thought you'd see the light."

"And what did you think, Sharpe?" Shelter asked.

"I thought," he replied, "of the gold."

"Who killed Sally?" Shelter asked suddenly, his mouth tightening.

"Not me." Sharpe held up his hands. "It must have been Peltier, I suppose. He knew you had come here to help Coral. Or he suspected it. He was a terribly violent man under all that soft pink flesh. But to return to what concerns me most, Captain, what are you going to do with me, if not kill me outright?"

"You should be turned over to the authorities. I imagine they'd be tickled to have the leader of the Tucson Gang under lock and key."

"Yes—but you can hardly take me in, can you? Not with a murder charge hanging over your head."

"I'll work it out. Maybe tie and gag you and throw you on the sheriff's doorstep—with the money bags from the Rembrandt job. Where is the money, by the way?"

"Downstairs. I have a wall safe."

"Let's get going then." Shelter motioned with the barrel of his pistol.

"Knowing you, there's no sense in offering you a cut, I don't suppose."

"None at all, Sharpe."

"Oh, well." Sharpe sighed, slapped his thighs and started to rise. "I'll need my hat," he said.

His hat was on the pillow of his bed, and he reached for it. And came up with a Smith and Wesson pistol. Sharpe spun and squeezed off three times, shattering the plaster at Shell's back, splintering the mirror, but Morgan had never taken his eyes off the man, never ceased to expect something. Sharpe was desperate and sooner or later he would have had to make some kind of a move.

Now he did, and he paid.

Shell stood, feet braced, eyes cold, face immobile and he touched off one round. The .44 slug buried itself in Able Sharpe's tortured face and he was slammed back, spattering the wall, his bed with blood.

Morgan's mouth tightened and he took a slow deep breath, fighting off the nervous muscular reaction. Sharpe was dead. Peltier was dead.

And it didn't matter in the least. There was a small, dark-eyed girl lying near death in a Rembrandt hotel room, and there was nothing Shelter Morgan and his guns could do about it.

He stepped to Sharpe's body and patted it down, coming up with a small iron key on a leather fob. Pocketing it, Shelter went out into the hallway, scanning its length. There was no one else in the house apparently, no one at least who wanted to advertise his presence. The shots might have been heard by the hands out at the breaking corral, but then again it was possible they had not. Shelter didn't intend to gamble on it anyway.

He moved swiftly to the head of the staircase and went down, four steps at a time. He looked through a door to find the kitchen—empty—retreated and found what he wanted—a library with a huge, terrible picture of a cattle drive on it.

Behind the painting was the safe.

The key fit and Shelter swung the round door of the safe open, watching over his shoulder, listening as he worked. The loot was in two canvas sacks still stencilled with the bank's name.

Shelter held them in his left hand, his Colt ready in his right. He had turned away from the safe when he heard the clamor at the front door, boots clattering across the wooden porch. He turned to the window, opened it and stepped out, rushing toward the oaks and the tethered gray horse as an excited shout went up from the house.

Reaching his horse, Shelter jammed the money sacks into his saddle bags and lit out through the trees, whipping the gray with his hat until they were clear of the oaks and out onto the empty pastureland.

No shots were fired, but Morgan didn't slow his pace until he was into the broken hills. Then he halted, wiping the sweat from his eyes, watching the backtrail until he was satisfied that the Rafter CB hands weren't on his track.

When the gray was rested Shelter turned it toward Rembrandt, feeling a strange sense of loss, an emptiness and a pang of sorrow as he thought of the woman still lying in bed, hovering on the brink of death.

But it was over. Peltier was dead. Able Sharpe had gone to join the rest of his battalion in the dark lands. Rembrandt would have its money returned so that seed corn could be purchased, someone's daughter have that wedding dress, the roof patched, that bull brought in.

He would have to move cautiously still—there was no way now of proving that he did not kill Sally. But he would return the money and then wait and watch. Wait until Coral Scant could rise from her bed, that warm smile in place, looking confidently toward the future, a future rich and bright.

That daydream was shattered before Morgan ever reached Rembrandt.

He could see them on the hill above the town and Shelter reined up, squinting as he studied them, his frown carved deeply. It looked like half the town of Rembrandt was on that slope picking up the scattered ore which had been lost when the freight wagon rolled.

And they weren't picking it up to return to Coral. There were people with sacks, men with wheelbarrows, three buckboards, kids with buckets, like a team of cotton pickers working across that slope and down into the gorge.

Shelter dismounted and sat cross-legged on the ground watching until darkness began to settle and the townspeople headed in to Rembrandt toting their booty.

He waited through the night until the town was dark and silent. There were only two lights burning in town, not counting the saloon. The hotel and the sheriff's office both had lamps shining in their windows.

That suited Morgan fine—those were the two places he meant to visit.

Tightening the cinches to the gray he swung aboard and headed toward Rembrandt, a silent, scowling man weighted down by his thoughts.

172

He left the gray in an alley and stashed the money bags behind a pile of trash. Then he slipped through the silent streets to the hotel. There was a light in Coral's window, a nurse sitting in the corner chair.

He went in through the window and the nurse came to her feet shrieking.

"Who are you! What do you want. Get out!"

"Take it easy, lady. I just want to see Miss Scant."

"Who are you! You get out or I'll call the sheriff!"

"It's all right," the weak voice said from the bed and Shelter turned to see Coral struggling to sit up. "He's a friend of mine. A very good friend."

Muttering, the nurse left the room, taking her knitting with her and Shell sat down on the bed next to Coral.

"How are you?"

"Oh, Shell . . ." inexplicably she burst into tears. Taking his hand she held it next to her cheek, kissing it before she let it go. She looked up at him with shining, moist eyes.

"You all right?" He wiped back a strand of dark hair from her pale forehead.

"I'm fine—now. It's just that I didn't know where you were. I couldn't remember what happened. I thought, imagined, the sheriff had taken you and that you were in jail. Or worse."

"Not hardly." He smiled again. "As a matter of fact I'm on my way to have a talk with the sheriff. I think we can get this all straightened out."

"Do you!" Her optimism quickly faded. "What are you going to do? Something dangerous?"

"No. That's all over. The fighting part."

She looked at him dubiously, her eyes asking questions which Shelter didn't answer. He didn't want to disturb her by telling her about Brunner and Peltier and so they sat there in silence for a long while.

"You'll be back at the mine in no time."

"Will I? I don't know, Shell. Can I go through that again?"

"That's up to you."

"I have a feeling—you wouldn't be there, would you?"

"You wouldn't need me," he said with a light smile.

"That's what I thought," she said miserably, closing her eyelids which were pale blue in the lamplight. "I don't care about that gold, Shell. Not now. I should have left it buried under that slide. I proved Father was right—that was all I wanted, I guess. Maybe I could show those ore samples to Triple X or one of the other big mining concerns and just sell the claim out."

"That's the best way to go if you don't want to work it," Shell agreed. He didn't tell her she had no samples, that the good citizens of Rembrandt had sacked it all. It wasn't all that important. If Triple X or one of the other big operators got a look at the claim Coral could sell and sell quickly. Maybe she was right to do so. Developing a claim took a lot of men and a lot of equipment. She had proven her point. But she was no miner—she was a young woman who deserved a decent home and an ordinary life.

Her hand felt slack and cool in his and looking down Morgan saw that she had fallen off to sleep. The nurse opened the door and stared with distaste at Morgan who rose, nodded and stepped out the window.

He had one more visit to make. And speaking to Sheriff Flowers wasn't going to be half so pleasant.

16.

Colin Flowers stretched massively, raising his arms over his head. He was in his chair, boots on the desk which was littered with reward posters. It was a moment before he realized that his front door had opened and someone had entered. And another long moment before he could make himself believe that what he saw was real.

"Morgan."

"Brought you something," Shell said. With one hand he tossed the money bags onto the sheriff's desk, sending posters fluttering.

"Jesus," Flowers breathed. "Is that what I think it is?"

"Only if you think it's the loot from last night's bank robbery." Shell moved to where the sheriff sat and eased his Colt from its well-oiled holster.

Flowers, to give him his due, took it coolly. He watched as Morgan sat on the bench next to the opposite wall, his pistol held loosely in hand.

"Why'd you come here? Where'd you get the

money? Just where in hell do you fit in, Morgan?"

"I'll tell you where I fit in. I came to Rembrandt looking for a no good, lying thieving bastard named Able Sharpe. I happened to fall in with a little girl named Coral Scant. For one of those two reasons I was set up. A girl was killed in my bed and I took off. Up in the hills Coral Scant reopened her father's claim. Some people didn't like that. They tried to kill me, did kill two other men."

"Who?"

"Walt Fogarty under the orders of Peltier."

"Fogarty. Yes," the sheriff said, "I can believe that. Walt's dead, you know."

"Is he?" Shelter asked expressionlessly.

"As a matter of fact, so's Peltier."

"Do tell."

"You don't know anything about that."

"Just what you've told me," Shell said. The sheriff nodded slightly. The corner of his mouth twitched.

"You robbed Peltier to get even," Flowers suggested.

"And then brought the money back? That doesn't make sense to me, does it to you?"

"No. Who then?"

"A man named Able Sharpe. The man who bossed the Tucson Gang up until a couple of years ago when a safe full of dynamite went up in his face. You know him as Carl Brunner."

"Brunner." Flowers didn't look surprised, only suddenly enlightened. "I guess I knew something was funny with Brunner's story of a steamboat boiler going up while he was riding the Rio Grande. I guess I should have known . . . I liked the man, Morgan."

176

"But you believe me?"

"I believe you," Flowers sighed. "That's where you got the money, is it? From Brunner."

"That's right."

"And Brunner?"

"He won't be coming to claim the money, Sheriff."

"You can put down the gun, Morgan."

"Can I?" Shell smiled wryly. "I've only got your word on that."

"Well luckily for you, I've got more than your word to go by." Flowers nodded his head and stood. "All right?"

"If you move easily."

"Come on then," he said. Reaching for a key ring hanging from a nail in the wall he opened the door to the cells. He led Shelter in and gestured toward a cell where Baker sat looking up at them with red eyes.

"Told you to keep riding," Shelter growled.

"You're lucky he didn't. He wanted whisky and he came after it. Had a little too much and started talking a little too much. When I got him in here he talked a hell of a lot more, didn't you Baker?"

"Go to hell," the outlaw murmured.

"He talked about Mister Peltier and about a crazy man with blue eyes going after the banker. He talked about Walt Fogarty and hitting the woman up in the hills, about Walt playing Apache. He talked about a certain other job. One where he and Walt killed a woman and left her there beside you."

Morgan felt the tension drain out of his neck and shoulders. He just stared at the sheriff, trying to decide if it was real. Baker's eyes told him it was and Morgan looked down at the gun in his hand and holstered it.

"Sorry, Morgan," Flowers said unexpectedly, and he seemed genuinely apologetic.

Shell asked him, "Why did you deny knowing who owns the Rafter CB brand."

"Because I've got a duty to protect my people, Morgan. That night I could see the fire in your eyes. I could imagine you riding out to that ranch and gunning down one of our leading citizens. I figured it was my job to look into that, not yours."

"It would have saved a lot of grief, Flowers. Your way was just too damned slow."

"The law usually is, Morgan. But I'm sworn to uphold it, and that's the way it is."

"All the laws?" Shell asked. They had come back into the sheriff's office, Flowers sagging down behind his desk again. His eyes narrowed at this question.

"What do you mean?"

"You know what happened this afternoon. Half the people in this town were up in the hills pocketing Coral Scant's ore."

"Doing her a favor, maybe."

"Yeah? Have they brought any in?"

"All right—it was wrong. Maybe. I'm not sure what the legalities would be. Salvaging that ore when the owner's abandoned it."

"Hell of a lot of choice she had about that!" Morgan flared up.

"Yeah, I know."

"But those people up there are the people who elected you and pay your salary."

"That's about right," Flowers admitted. "They're also neighbors and friends. You know what I've got?"

The sheriff leaned forward, clasping his hands on his desk. "By the time they split that rock up they've got next to nothing. What I've got is maybe a hundred petty thieves—as you say, the people who elected me. Now just how in blazes am I supposed to arrest them all, jail them? You think our judge is going to hear the cases? What cases! Who's going to testify anyway? You—against the whole town. That's the spot I'm in, and whether I like it or not—and it happens I don't, it stinks—that' the way it's got to be. The girl's all right?" Shell nodded, and Flowers added, "She should count herself lucky."

Morgan stood silently for a long while, looking at the sheriff across the dimly lighted room.

"Flowers," he said finally, "I don't think I like this little community of yours."

"No one's making you stay."

"No, and no one's making me leave," Shelter said with rising anger.

"If you mean me, I don't intend to. If you mean the town—well, I'd keep my mouth shut about them being a pack of thieves if I was you."

"Would you?" Shelter stared coldly at the lawman. "I guess you would. Tell me, Sheriff. What's the limit for petty larceny around here?"

"You mean when is it grand theft? Anything fifty dollars or under is petty larceny."

Shelter crossed to the money bags, opened one and removed fifty dollars, showing it to the sheriff. Then he threw the sack down and walked out the door, leaving Flowers to sit thoughtfully behind his desk, feeling just a little bit smaller than he had when the tall man came in.

Morgan walked the gray to the stable and roused Pedro from his sleep.

"Señor!" the stable hand recoiled in alarm.

"It's all right, Pedro. Everything's cleared up. I'm just a petty thief like everyone else."

"Señor?"

"Never mind." Morgan gave Pedro the fifty dollars. "For the use of the gray," he said. The stable-hand looked goggle-eyed at the money.

"It is far too much."

"All right. Listen, then. Bring me some breakfast in the morning out of that money. I can't remember the last full meal I've had. And I want to use your loft."

"To sleep?"

"To sleep." The weariness was settling, the soreness in joints and muscle accumulated over the past days was wearing. He wanted only to sleep, to rest, to forget it all. He climbed to the loft and was asleep in minutes in the sweet-smelling hay.

Over, he thought before he dropped off. It's all over.

He couldn't have been more wrong.

Pedro had breakfast ready when Shell awakened, yawning, in the morning and clambered down from the loft. It looked like fifty dollars worth of food to Morgan. Pedro had brought eggs with tortillas stirred in, a quart pot of coffee, three thick slabs of fried ham, some golden brown potatoes, and Shell settled in. There might have been a bite of something left when he was finished. If there was it was only because he couldn't find it.

He washed in the tack room, using a barrel of cold water and a bar of strong yellow lye soap. He wanted to be clean and shaven when he next saw Coral. Come to think of it, she had never seen him just that way.

A new shirt would have been nice, but he would have to make do. Borrowing thread and needle from Pedro he patched the torn dark blue shirt he had been wearing as well as possible.

Then feeling human for the first time in a while he saddled the gray and went out into the bright sunshine, the empty main street of Rembrandt.

Shell paused, frowning. There was no one around. Absolutely no one! He shrugged and walked to the hotel. Coral looked fine and well, much stronger.

"I wrote a letter to Triple X," she told him. They're going to send a man down to look at the claim.

"Then what?"

"I don't know. Back to Indiana, perhaps." She was silent and thoughtful for a moment. Perhaps there was another man back there. She looked at Morgan with a touch of sheepishness.

"Well, it worked out well enough," Morgan said.

"Did it? If you don't think of Alejandro, of Paco, of the other men who died, it did. None of it was really worth it, Shell. Not really."

He didn't argue with her. They talked of other things for an hour until the nurse ran him out.

Emerging from the hotel Shelter looked up and down the street. He saw two people. A man of nearly ninety sitting in front of the general store which was locked up, and a kid with a fishing pole and a straw hat tilted back on his head.

Shelter stopped the kid.

"Where's everybody at, son?"

The kid looked at him as if he was crazy. "The gold

181

strike, mister! Everybody in town's gone out to it. My Ma and Pa and two brothers. Me, I'd rather fish. Digging for gold sounds like work."

"What gold strike?" Shelter asked coldly. The kid's grin fell away and he backed off.

"I don't know. I don't know anything," he said, then he took off at a run, bare feet devouring ground. Shelter crossed to the sheriff's office, but it was locked up.

Scowling he stepped into the gray's saddle and started at a walk out of Rembrandt. He knew already, had known, should have know much sooner. The gold strike—Coral Scant's claim.

He recalled the townsmen he had heard a few nights back discussing that. Talking about how easy it would be to follow the wagon tracks back and find the mine. Now they had done it.

Nothing much, Coral had told him, kept Rembrandt alive. The timber was gone, the old strikes played out. It was a hungry, dying town. A greedy town. A thieving one.

Morgan heeled the gray into a gallop and headed out of town and up into the hills. Following their sign was no problem. Wagons, horses, men and women on feet. It was like a vast migration. An entire town setting out toward Coral Scant's claim while she lay sick abed.

Shell kicked the gray into a run, his teeth clenched, not quite believing any of this. And where in hell was Sheriff Flowers? Looking the other away, of course. Can't bring them all to trial, the lawman had said.

Maybe not. But they could all come to judgement. Shelter Morgan style.

He crossed the mesa at mid-day, the hot sun beating down, a dry wind out on the desert lifting sand, forming erratic dust devils.

Long before he got to the canyon he heard them. Heard the ringing of pick and stone, the yelling and cursing. It was as if a madness had taken over the people of Rembrandt—gold fever. Not only did they have to have that gold, but they had to have it now. They had to be first before anyone else got there.

Shelter reined up and looked down the dusty canyon, disbelief clinging to him. Men dragged sackloads of ore from the mine. Women, their skirts tucked up into their waistbands, sorted it, hauled it to waiting horses and mules. Others—near-grown kids mostly, stood watch over the gold with rifles, jealously stealing glances at their neighbors.

It was an anthill alive with gold hungry madmen. Shelter started on down, circling wide to come up behind the claim.

"Hold it!" a man with a gray beard popped up out of a clump of brush. He had a burlap bag of gold ore by his feet. The ore had burst the bag and he had been trying to collect it again when Shelter came up on him.

"Turn tail, stranger. This is mine, and all of that down below is claimed."

"You're damned right it is," Morgan said. The bearded townsman gestured with his rifle again.

"Scoot, I said. We want no outsiders in here."

"You know you're trespassing," Shell said. "Trespassing, stealing from a registered claim. Now threatening me with a rifle. You know that." He leaned forward, staring into the townsman's strained eyes. "You're nothing but a thief, mister."

For a moment the man's eyes clouded over, suddenly they cleared, anger shining brightly in them. "That's bull shit. Get out of here, I'm warning you. They won't take kindly to your presence down below."

With complete disdain Shelter nudged the gray's flanks and rode over the man's stolen ore, practically over him. The townsman who had thievery in his heart, but not murder, fell back, grumbling and cursing.

Shelter came down onto the claim a minute later. No one looked up. They were as busy as squirrels. Off to the south, toward the gorge two men had fallen into a fist fight. Shell saw two kids no higher than his waist contending over a piece of ore.

A woman screamed at her man to hurry up. An ancient claim jumper sat in the shade of a big rock, holding his chest after working himself into exhaustion and maybe a heart attack.

Shelter stepped down, slid his rifle from the scabbard and mounted a ledge. Still no one paid any attention to him until he cut loose, firing three shots from the Winchester into the air.

They halted abruptly. Hands filled with ore, faces turned up to Morgan. He looked them over coldly for a long minute before saying:

"Get the hell out of here, all of you! You're trespassing on private property. This is a legally registered claim belonging to Miss Coral Scant!"

"Who're you!" a belligerent red-headed man shouted.

"I work for Miss Scant. And I'm telling you to get out of here."

184

A buzz went through the gathered townspeople as they discussed it. A kid winged a rock at Shelter. It pinged off the ledge and rattled down into the gorge.

"We ain't leaving!" the red-headed man shouted finally.

"You're not." Shell nodded. "Want me to tell you what I think of you?" He let his eyes rake them one by one. Some of the women had to turn their eyes down, their heads away. But mostly they just stared back challengingly. He was the interloper. He was the troublemaker. They stood together—if they were all doing it, it was right.

"A woman's lying sick in bed right now," Shelter told them all. "Coral Scant. I guess most of you know her. This is her property. What you're doing is exactly the same as rushing into the home of a dying man and stripping it clean. I don't know, maybe that's the way you folks do things around here. Maybe you leave a funeral and go to that person's house to see what you can cart off."

An angry shout went up, and Shell tried to figure what it reminded him of. Then he had it—once he had heard an angry sound like that directed at him. It was the sound of a lynch mob, an angry, defensive bunch of people knowing they were wrong, banding together to convince themselves they were right, ready to trample down anyone who stood before them to tell them they were wrong.

"You better just turn tail, mister," someone said.

"What's he going to do? Shoot us all?"

"Get out! You ain't the law."

Another rock was winged his way and Shelter just stood looking down at them, knowing it was no good.

What *was* he going to do, as the man had demanded, shoot them all? Arrest them? Stand in front of the mine shaft? If he had had dynamite with him, he knew what he would have done. Closed that shaft for good and all.

He looked into their faces now, knowing that no argument would change their minds. They were gold hungry, wild-eyed with the thought of riches.

"I'll see that this doesn't pay," Shelter warned them. "I'll repeat it: this isn't your property. Get out of here, go home. The money from the bank robbery has been recovered, if that carries any weight with some of you who need money desperately enough to do what you're doing."

"I think you'd better drift," someone said and Shell saw the rifle in his hands, the rifles in the hands of a dozen of these good, honest citizens.

"I've asked you," Shell said. "Now, I'm telling you—get!"

No one moved. Someone snickered.

"You get, mister. We're here and we're staying. If you or anyone else tries to stop us, he's a dead man!"

Shelter, looking into the face of the crowd, believed it. It was hopeless. He turned away sharply, to the sound of laughter, walked to his horse and swung aboard, riding out of the canyon without ever once looking back.

17.

The town remained empty for a week. There was a tent town going up out at the claim. Two men had been killed squabbling over gold. Shelter had this from Sheriff Flowers who looked about ready to throw in his badge and turn to honest work.

Coral had been unaware of any of this. It didn't seem the time to cause her worry. She had been ill and was not strong. By the end of that week, however, she was up and out of bed, looking well if not entirely spry.

"I know," she told Morgan one morning.

"You know?" Shell sat on Coral's bed while she stood before the mirror, patting her hair into place. "About what, Coral?"

"The mine. The people out there."

"Who told you?"

"The representative Triple X Mines sent down here."

"He was out there, was he?"

"He was. It didn't stop him from closing a deal with

187

me. Most of the ore is along that deep vein, he said. And they'll never get at it with picks and shovels. Though he wasn't very happy about there being a tribe of squatters out there."

"But you did sign with Triple X."

"Signed and been paid."

She was suddenly aware of Shelter Morgan's body next to hers. His hand slipped around her waist and she leaned her head back against his chest. Shell studied her in the mirror. She looked weary, but her eyes were bright, alert, her smile came more easily now.

"Well, I suppose it worked out. There's only the promise I made to the people of Rembrandt left."

"The promise?" Coral turned, her eyes puzzled.

"I promised them they'd not profit by their thievery, by taking advantage of a very lovely woman—" it was necessary here for Morgan to pause and kiss one round, pink ear, the slope of Coral's neck "who was sick in bed."

"And just what did you mean by that?" she asked him.

"By the kiss?"

"That, I know. The promise, I mean. The threat."

"I don't know. Maybe I'll think of something."

"Maybe you already have," Coral whispered. The tiny kisses had caused a flush to creep up in her face. Now she turned and hugged Shell tightly. "When we get to Socorro."

"Is that where we're going?"

"It is. Because that's where the first stagecoach out of Rembrandt is going. And, Shelter Morgan, I've had enough of this town and its ways. I want to leave,

188

to go out into the wide world and see what awaits a young woman of some means."

"A bunch of men who'll make love to you for hope of some of that money is what awaits you," Shell said.

"And you?"

"Hell, I'd never take money, Coral."

"Damn me! Beg pardon, ma'am," the stage driver said, mopping his forehead as the hot yellow sun beat down. Coral nodded her forgiveness. "This is the craziest place I've ever been in. Look up and down the street. There's nobody here. I had to hitch my own horses. The dispatcher's gone. Wanted a beer and found the saloon closed. Wanted a plug of tobacco and found the general store locked up.

"A tall man with blue eyes came along and saw me there. He cracks the glass with his pistol, opens the door bold as you please and tosses me this plug before he walks around, picking up blankets and kerosene. I left a dime for the plug and scatted.

"Well, ready, are you?"

"In a minute," Coral Scant said. "There was another passenger."

"All right." The driver shrugged and leaned against the stagecoach wheel, muttering "Damndest thing." He straightened up suddenly. "Well, there he is—look at that, would you?"

And Coral, prim in long gray dress and gray bonnet, hand luggage firmly in her grip, turned to see Shelter Morgan crossing the road with an armload of blankets and a can of kerosene.

"Now what in hell is he up to?"

Shelter who had crossed to the alley beside the saloon placed down two blankets. As he had done across the street at the general store he saturated the blankets with kerosene, splashing a little on the walls. Then, as he had done at the bank, at the hotel, he struck a match with his thumb and tossed it onto the kerosene-soaked blanket and walked away, his face grim.

"Ready?" he asked, reaching the stage.

"I'm ready," the driver said a little nervously.

Then the tall man helped the young woman aboard and the Socorro stage pulled out, the driver snapping his whip above the ears of the team. As he made his run up the main street, he thought he saw smoke rising from behind the general store and again from beside the bank. He urged his horses on even faster. Rembrandt was plain spooky, and he wanted to be out of there, back to his family in Socorro.

He never turned to look back. Had he, minutes later he would have seen the waves of crimson flame sweeping through the empty buildings, smoke wafting into the crystal blue sky as Rembrandt paid for what it had stolen.

FORGE AHEAD IN **THE SCOUT** SERIES
BY BUCK GENTRY

#7: PRAIRIE BUSH (1110, $2.50)

Red-headed Melissa, an Army general's daughter, is in good hands with the Scout. And when they learn that her father has been kidnapped, she offers to help the Scout in any way she can—making this Holten's most sizzling adventure ever!

#8: PAWNEE RAMPAGE (1161, $2.50)

When the Scout finds himself at war with the entire Pawnee nation—to avenge the death of his Sioux bride—who can blame him for finding solace in the arms of a sumptuous lady journalist who's doing a piece on the frontier?

#9: APACHE AMBUSH (1193, $2.50)

Eli Holten has his hands full while scouting for a wagon train down the Santa Fe trail: his client runs the most famous "sporting house" in St. Louis, and she's moving it—lock, stock, and twenty girls!

#10: TRAITOR'S GOLD (1209, $2.50)

There's a luscious red-head who's looking for someone to lead her through the Black Hills of the Dakotas. And one look at the Scout tells her she's found her man—for whatever job she has in mind!

Available wherever paperbacks are sold, or order direct from the Publisher. Send cover price plus 50¢ per copy for mailing and handling to Zebra Books, 475 Park Avenue South, New York, N.Y. 10016 DO NOT SEND CASH.

THE HOTTEST SERIES IN THE WEST CONTINUES!

GUNN #14: THE BUFF RUNNERS (1093, $2.25)
Gunn runs into two hell-raising sisters caught in the middle of a buffalo hunter's feud. He hires out his sharpshooting skills—and doubles their fun!

GUNN #15: DRYGULCHED (1142, $2.25)
When Gunn agrees to look after a dying man's two lovely daughters, he finds himself having to solve a poaching problem too. And he's going to have to bring peace to the mountains—before he can get any himself!

GUNN #16: WYOMING WANTON (1196, $2.25)
Wrongly accused of murder, Gunn needs a place to lay low and plan his proof of innocence. And—when the next body turns up—pretty Mary is his only alibi. But will she lay her reputation on the line for Gunn?

BACK IN STOCK!

GUNN #1: DAWN OF REVENGE (1149, $2.25)

GUNN #2: MEXICAN SHOWDOWN (1150, $2.25)

GUNN #3: DEATH'S HEAD TRAIL (1182, 2.25)

GUNN #4: BLOOD JUSTICE (1183, $2.25)

Available wherever paperbacks are sold, or order direct from the Publisher. Send cover price plus 50¢ per copy for mailing and handling to Zebra Books, 475 Park Avenue South, New York, N.Y. 10016. DO NOT SEND CASH.